T0007543

BECAUSE

BECAUSE

a Novel

Andrew Steinmetz

ESPLANADE BOOKS

THE FICTION IMPRINT AT VÉHICULE PRESS

Published with the generous assistance of the Canada Council for
the Arts and the Canada Book Fund of the Department of
Canadian Heritage.

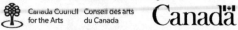

ESPLANADE EDITIONS EDITOR: DIMITRI NASRALLAH
Cover design by David Drummond
Set in Minion and Gill Sans by Simon Garamond
Printed by Marquis Imprimeur

Author's royalties are being donated to Girls+ Rock Ottawa

Copyright © Andrew Steinmetz 2023
All rights reserved.

Dépôt légal, Library and Archives Canada and the
Bibliothèque national du Québec, second trimester 2023

Published by Véhicule Press, Montréal, Québec, Canada
www.vehiculepress.com

Distribution in Canada by LitDistCo
www.litdistco.ca

Distribution in the U.S. by Independent Publishers Group
ipgbook.com

Printed in Canada on FSC®-certified paper.

Being young is a kind of stardom with some people

ANDREW O'HAGAN

Ain't it funny how you feel when you're findin' out it's real?

NEIL YOUNG

Any constraint is part of the skeleton that you build the composition on—including your own incompetence

BRIAN ENO

The name of this band is Because. That's what we're called. Because.
Why?
Because.
Because why?
Because we fuckin' told you so.

Prologue

1995

A rising star.

That's how you described him, this young kid who happened to have a weekly gig at a bar down the hill from the hospital. News spread around the city in the music press and by word of mouth that aficionados had to get themselves down there to see him perform. This kid, the prodigal son, the chosen one. The café was his testing ground. It was snowing when we left that evening and, inside the taxi, sitting side by side but windows apart, the strangest feeling caught in my chest. It was early December. Downtown was aglow, every tall building illuminated.

Well, he had a knack for it. Rufus already was a legend. An eccentric talent. And all of us musicians who converged in front of his piano understood that soon he'd blast our sorry souls to smithereens on his way up the charts. He was heavenly. He was going to be a star. One day we'd be able to say, "We knew him when…" It was like being party to some wunderkind solo-jam session: a five-year-old Diego Maradona ambling matador-like through the market juggling guavas on his left foot. We were privileged just to be there. Not a cliché: Rufus was born immersed in melody. His parents were musicians. His aunts and sister too. The family had musical genius, but Rufus was the flamboyant fairy child, this kid who tickled the ivories and smoked Gauloises and deconstructed one Chopin nocturne after another Satie experiment. It was Montreal casual. It was made for us. He wore a shabby baby-blue Adidas tracksuit. Bright white sneakers. The sideburns outweighed him. His caustic humour was endearing. Between sets of Thelonious Monk and Bill Evans, he gulped chocolate milk. And finally got a kick out of Dave Brubeck. "I'd like to rondo that ole Turk myself," he might have said, or something equally disparaging-sounding but true.

And then, after the Chopin, Satie, Monk, and Evans, he announced, "This is my junk."

His own junk was heartbreaking. His junk was operatic and bombastic. His junk was solid gold. He sold it with a teasing growl of snickering self-derision. And it was sturdy. But bittersweet. Songs so well-crafted you could pick them out of the air and put them down on the floor and sit on them. Melody so natural and complex that try as the evil genius might he could not ruin them. And ruin them he did try. But it was pointless. They would endure. His voice like any tool of genius broke consensus: you loved it or it made you want to claw at your ears. Spit, you loved his voice. I did too. Yes. It made him a less frightening angel. Made him more human.

It was getting late. Towards the end of the last set, he was in the habit of inviting a few friends and family to join him on stage. He got up from the piano. Sauntered over to the mike stand. His mom Kate held an accordion to her chest. Aunt went to the piano. His sister Martha on guitar. Rufus leaned into the microphone and said, "This is a sad event."

We stared at each other. Surprised. You and me.

"This last number is for the conehead lovers at the table in the front, and for all the misfits from outer space who are travelling through." My skin tingled. Your face flushed. "Also…" He swayed and rocked at the microphone. "…this marks my last gig, the last time you'll be able to see our show live here at the café. Directly following tonight's performance, my family is going to sneak out the back and cross the mountains and escape to Switzerland. I mean, New York."

The cast performed "Edelweiss" as an encore. We didn't know whether to laugh or cry. Rufus led his sister by hand off the stage, and we left the café and outside hailed a cab, got in, and the taxi took us straight up the mountain to the hospital. It was everything we could ask for, Spit. An evening to never forget.

WE FORM A BAND

Summer 1981

I'm letting it be. On the roof playing guitar when Uncle Per enters the backyard by the side gate and waves hello and climbs the ladder.

"I won't come any further." Just his head showing. "Shit, it's hot up here."

"I'm in the shade."

"Stay where you are."

No other plans.

"Hey, what's this I heard about you starting a band with Transformer?"

"Who told you?"

"Your mother. Do you have a name yet?"

"Because."

Uncle Per scratches his ear.

"Because, eh. What kind of music?"

"Loud."

"Whatever you feel like, right?"

"I guess."

"I'll tell you what. Take my records, my whole collection."

Sounds of silence.

"For inspiration, I mean... I don't listen to them anymore."

"What do you have?"

"A bit of everything." He looks across the roof to the road. Takes the lay of the land from up high. Three cars in line at the Stop sign. Knock-out drivers in Dorval.

"Where's your mother anyway?"

"With Transformer."

"Isn't it Thursday?"

Meaning, shouldn't one of us be out delivering the newspaper? We share a route that zigzags this side of the highway towards the lake: fifty houses, apartment buildings too.

"Yeah." We did the route earlier though.

"Sister at work?"

"With the vets."

"Good for her. That's great."

What is this, roll call with uncle? He notices the cigarette pegged at the butt end of my guitar. A trick of the trade learned yesterday. And points at it.

"You shouldn't smoke."

But he does. Morfar too.

"You're still young."

"Not forever."

Scratches that itch again.

"That's true."

Everything settled, Uncle Per descends the ladder and tickles the gate's latch to disappear into his car, and he's gone.

BECAUSE

We formed two weeks ago to play our acoustic guitars, presents from Mom for just about passing the school year. Identical and made from soft blond wood, our instruments stink like glue and have no heft when we lift them by the neck and step to the front of the mirror. Look at us: skinny and pale. Bare arms are it. Black jeans fit like rust. I repeatedly get into some difficulty sitting cross-legged in mine. "Tell me about it," Transformer says. "I can't zip up without causing a full-blown riot."

The summer is spent jamming upstairs in our shared bedroom. Bjorn Borg and Patti Smith posters on Transformer's side, Neil Young and the Expos pennant on mine. Twin beds against opposite walls, cheap headboards etched with penknives by the crazies counting our locked-up days. I play left-handed. Transformer noodles as I strum. There is a caste system. Lead and rhythm. No union but there are ciggy breaks. Take fives when silence reigns through smoke rings. Music is sacred and sacrificing, and making it is lonely. It ought to be privately sickening. We remain quiet about the endeavour—Transformer does, and I do.

Transformer stares out the window like an indoor cat and bites his bottom lip. Transformer is sixteen, going on fifteen. With curly hair and blue eyes, he's the misfit of the group.

"We gotta *do* something."

He runs his hand through his hair, fingers taut in Vs.

The hand, the hair—the sign to get back to work. More guitar and gut longing. More thrashing around in the dark. More agonizing immanence.

I strum bastard chords, and Transformer hangs his head over the fretboard. His eyes are tightly closed. He's not even watching where he's going.

INCANTATION

"In the beginning was Because, and the band Because was good, and all songs by Because were opiates for the people."

"What are you talking about?"

No reply.

"What are opiates?"

Still no reply. I'm a bother. He ignores me in favour of his mirror image, a doppelganger full of surprises. It will keep him busy.

Minutes later, Transformer is at it again: "The name of this band is Because for Now. That's what we're called."

"Why are you changing it? I don't like *for Now*."

"Who cares what you think."

Transformer has a point. Who cares? Nobody. Voicing an opinion is new. It's treacherous. This thespian is a proud snot with only one routine. During the day, he forces me to rehearse with him in front of the mirror—repetition is key to getting the feel and our timing right.

"The name of this band…"

To bring the house down: strumming hard on wooden guitars out of tune. Screaming ourselves senseless.

INHERITANCE

T Rex. Donavan. Ten Years After. Joan Baez. CSNY. Lots of Rolling Stones. The Beatles. Canned Heat. The Byrds. The Yardbirds. Eagles. Janis Joplin. Bob Dylan. Black Sabbath. Pink Floyd. The Who. The Kinks. Cream. The Moody Blues. Genesis. Elton John. Some ELO. Jimi Hendrix. Deep Purple.

A bunch of hippie dung and a bit of metal with a sprinkle of records from the first British invasion. Uncle Per brings them over, loaded into a brown suitcase. Comes right up the stairs and enters our room. Wearing a white jumpsuit and looking like the kind of mechanic who, in lieu of working on four cylinders, polishes disco balls for a living.

"This is your inheritance, boys. They're all in pretty good condition."

"Thanks, Uncle Per."

"Yeah—" Transformer slips a finger down his throat. "Tack."

"You sure you don't need them?" The youngest is born redundant.

"*Nobody* needs them," Transformer says.

"Like I said, I don't listen to them anymore, and since you two are starting a band…"

"Any bootlegs?"

"You wish." Transformer shuts down my little-brother optimism. But here I am, on the floor like a toddler in a sandbox surrounded by forty LPs, already picking and sorting. Not him though. Seated on the edge of the bed, Transformer nudges *Tumbleweed Connection* with his toe.

"Sorry. No bootlegs. But there's a lot of good music here," Uncle Per declares, surveying his old records fanned out on the floor. "Go ahead, put something on. Anything."

"Nah." I'm not going to. I never listen to new music when somebody's in the room with me. It's pure torture. What if I don't like it?

"Just pick something. What about you, Transformer?"

Vigorous headshake from the conscientious objector.

Uncle Per sighs. "I'll let you two get back to work." Lifts the empty suitcase. "I hope you take some time to discover your roots." And leaves us alone.

Transformer is left astounded by our new fortune, skeptical but finally entranced by an isosceles triangle emitting a prism of light and multi-coloured spaceships aplenty. A kaleidoscope of album art showing a weird slice of life, including a foursome in cream jumpsuits captaining a helicopter. We're familiar with the natty brat with walking stick arranged before a piano for his greatest hits. Less so with the nonchalant legends who have gone and taken a leak against a concrete monolith because it was there. No surprise in the reprise of four familiar faces peering down at us from the fab height of the sixties, but what about this psychedelic gypsy soul who inquires of us, *Are You Experienced*? No, we are not experienced. We are just looking.

"That was all bullshit," Transformer says.

"What?"

"His speech about roots." There was no speech. "The roots tangle and strangle." Transformer is miffed. Disdain curls his lower lip. "Roots are rot."

"I guess."

"I mean it." Blows out his cheeks. "Since when is old music more important than what's happening right now?"

Uncle Per didn't mean it that way. He didn't.

QUAGMIRE

The summer is slow murder. A quagmire of months. The room turns soupy. When it gets boiling inside, we grab our guitars, hop onto the desk, and exit through the window onto the veranda roof. There's a big maple to the side of the house—we edge over, bony asses gripping the gentle slope into the partial shade. The shingles are rough. While I pick pellets from my palm, Transformer flicks a lit cigarette down onto the lawn. At night, when sparks fly, that's what we call our light show.

"Let's play," Transformer says.

A little dazed after hours jamming inside, I strum softly, whispering nasty, sweet junk.

"Hold up. What was that?" Transformer points.

"G, maybe."

"Good." Transformer nods that he's got it. But he doesn't. The name of the chord makes no real difference—we don't know our chords. Still, as if to be polite, we always ask: *What chord?*

"Don't stop playing."

"But that's all I have."

"And sing it this time."

"Sing what?"

In my defence, I don't really sing. I just say things.

"Just keep going. Go into the chorus here," Transformer declares — but is he serious? Too late. Abruptly the wheels come off, and we hit a wall. I go flying one way, he goes flying in the other.

That song is dead.

SUPINE

A little later, back inside the cauldron, supine travellers, resting from here to eternity.

"I hope at least I'm adopted," Transformer says.

"What do you mean?"

"I was just thinking."

"But you weren't."

Silence ticks.

"How can you tell?"

"Because you have Morfar's eyes."

The mirror is only a narrow strip on the closet door. No way we look alike. Not with his curls and blue eyes. But adoption is flawed, wishful thinking. Transformer again challenges his gaunt doppelganger, showing off in a T-shirt strung together with safety pins.

"What if I don't want to look like him?" His guitar hangs very low.

"You do and you don't. Don't worry. Morfar's eighty-one!"

"How do you remember everything?"

Easy. Morfar was born on New Year's Eve at the turn of the century. I remember that while Transformer slashes at his guitar.

"The name of this band is Because." Down strum chops again. "That's what we're called."

From stage left, I say, "Do we have to do this again?"

"Why not?"

Because it's fucking stupid.

"Just come here." Transformer gestures. "From the top."

It's a squeeze to share the spotlight, but we've rehearsed this a thousand times.

"The name of this band is Because."

"*Why?*" Leaning into view, hands cupping my megaphone mouth.

"Because."

"Because why?"

"BECAUSE WE FUCKIN' TOLD YOU MORONS SO."

VISITOR

Occasionally we get a visitor. Usually our mother, Flowers.

"Don't you ever leave this place?"

"It's our room."

"At least open the window."

Transformer sighs, leans his guitar against the chair. We've been jamming since mid-morning. Nothing was happening. But she's right, effort is pungent.

"You really should try to get outside today."

"We're in a band," Transformer reminds her.

"Maybe you need lessons?"

He stares at his crotch.

She turns to her youngest. "It's sunny out."

"He knows that already," Transformer says. "He's pretty smart."

Mom gives me that special look: *Does he always talk for you?*

Truth is, it is a comfort of some kind that he speaks for us both. That way I won't say anything dense.

I tell Flowers, "We went outside. We had a smoke on the roof not that long ago."

"That's what every mother wants to hear."

We are spending so much time on the roof this summer

that Flowers bought a ladder and had it tied down to use as a fire escape. Transformer doesn't buy the explanation. He's paranoid people are spying on us. Personally, I view it as an omen.

"Why not go to the swimming pool?"

Now she's pushing it. Usually when Flowers delivers laundry, she wades in, basket on hip, and steps to the dresser, where she drops a volcano heap on the floor. It's only when she pauses at the door on her way out, because she wants to talk, that we cut the noise and the music drains out of the room.

"The pool?" Transformer points at the side of his head. "With *this* hair?"

Flowers rubs her forehead. He's about to make a joke at the expense of Mormor, who is a bit of a fanatic about our appearance.

"Do you think they'd let me in looking like this?"

The hair reference dates from the time we were in elementary school. Before leaving for school, Mormor would hunt us down with a comb in her teeth. She usually caught me before I could make it out the door. She would bend and take the comb from her teeth, and for a moment that made me worry she might slit my throat, but instead she'd only spit on the teeth and drag it through my hair. Plus, she talked at me in Swedish—which is a language I still don't understand—while just wiping down my bangs with a soft palm to finish the deal. I really didn't mind it that much. Eventually, Morfar would appear from down the hallway to scoff at her efforts before pleading with her to let me go at once so I wouldn't be late for school.

Flowers ignores Transformer and his antics, as she calls them. In time she says, "The DRA must be doing something special for Canada Day. Are your friends going?" The Dorval Recreation Association is what she is talking about, not the Dorval Republican Army. And anyone who has taken swimming lessons at the city pool knows it as the Drown Right Away. Including us.

"We're not going."

She checks in with her youngest again. "Don't you want to go to the pool?"

Me? Because why? Because since I'm fourteen I still might get excited by the idea of jumping in a septic tank overpopulated with six-year-olds? Last summer, we spent quite a lot of time at the Drown Right Away. But last summer we hadn't formed the band. In the changing rooms, kids the age of ten and under get really strange in the showers. Without pubic hair everyone gets nervous. Today no one in the band is going to the pool for Canada Day. It wouldn't be good for our image. Besides, we like it inside our room, where it's humid and the walls are close, where all day long we can soak up our own music.

"Well, I tried."

"Anything else?" Transformer reaches for his guitar. "We're not budging from this place. Don't worry, Flowers, we like it in here. We're just incubating."

She winces, doesn't she, but the fact is we need more time alone.

Some clean-up time. Sorting through the inheritance. We're panning for gold, sleeve by album sleeve.

"Looksee here." Transformer discovers the centrefold stuffed into a Black Sabbath album cover. He opens wide—whistles—and flips Miss April into my lap.

"What should I do with it?"

"Use your head."

"Funny."

"My guess is," Transformer muses, while orientating himself to the album art of *Paranoid*, "that Uncle Per used to incubate to this. I heard it's quite solid."

"Let's put it on," I say.

He goes ahead and gives it a spin. While it plays, I become distracted by something else I heard about our uncle recently.

"Do you really think Uncle Per likes disco now?"

"In the first place, Panny... you can't just casually ask a question like that. Out of the blue."

Panny. A name that goes way back.

"Why not?"

"Because."

Set up. Joke. Transformer's the master—but seriously. I want to know.

"Does Uncle Per go dancing?"

"Probably, yeah. By helicopter or something. He goes to the Edgewater." Transformer holds *Arrival* square in my face. Exhibit A: crammed inside the glass cockpit, the ABBA men resemble kittens. "Although, I bet he didn't intend to give us *this*." He tosses the ABBA record. "His loss."

"Maybe we should return it to him?"

ABBA and even Miss April, but keep Black Sabbath.

"If punk was the dark side of the seventies—disco is the vomit side."

What side are we on? I wonder.

More time will tell.

PANNY

The name hearkens back to the summers we played a primitive game called chase with the next-door Willey twins. As the youngest, I chased after the others until I was out of breath. I'd turn the corner of the house in my gym shorts to discover they'd climbed the apple tree and were already in position, high in the crown, ready to hold me off. If I reached up and got hold of a branch, they'd stamp on my fingers. At the same time, they'd shout about Sasquatch and the killer bees coming to get me. "Help me up, help me up," I'd plead. "Help me get up." But there was no chance of that, and when I'd start bawling, they'd pelt me with crab apples and start singing my theme song:

"Yes, Mr. Panny is our man, he's so full of gasoline that he's always, always clean!"

Their voices distinctly gung-ho. "Yes, Mr. Panny!" the refrain would make me drop to the ground on my side.

"What's wrong, Mr. Panny?" came the inquiry from up high.

"He's scared of dying."

"You scared?"

I'd sob then with a sickness that made them laugh berserk.

"You're not going to die, stupid…"

We're just teasing you, Mr. Panny.

PIGS

We brothers dig. We're like pigs. We dig with angst and anger. We dig with the spirit of nicotine. We dig to reach the stars with out-of-tune guitars.

Sooner or later, we shall unearth history.

We are owed something.

For the record, our first original is "Fuck Creation."

Verses: G to A times three.

Chorus: G to A.

For the record, we destroyed the way into our creation song.

Look out!

We're coming!

Noise is our signal.

Fuck Creation will destroy you!

Transformer has an amplifier now, and a second-hand Strat. I'm still digging with my old acoustic. When we jam, I can't hear myself. He's too loud.

I complain, but Transformer won't have it.

"Too bad," he says, "it's our new sound."

Transformer noodles while I shout gibberish at the top of my lungs.

"Turn up," Transformer says.

"I can't."

"Then don't complain."

Transformer turns away into the music. He might be smiling; I'm never sure. My fingers are raw. Blistered from these thick-gauge wire strings.

I'm losing this battle of the band, and it's stupid.

We only play what we write. We are not prolific. But we are devout. Though being the co-founders of the group, sharing all responsibility, takes its toll.

"I'm tired of it all," Transformer says.

"Of what?"

"Everything."

The battle of Because? The paparazzi? Is it exhausting to be playing our originals over and over and never going outside? We have three songs: "People Disease," "Grey Weather," and the sentimental hit "Fuck Creation."

"You should learn some minor chords," Transformer wearily informs me.

"What about you?"

"Not my bag."

Transformer stumbles like a wreck to the mirror. "We need a better look. Get up. Bring your guitar and stand beside me."

I go to him reluctantly, feeling old-fashioned with this wooden box bouncing off my chest.

"Don't hold it like an accordion," Transformer scowls and adjusts the strap, "not so high," leaning over me like Mormor fixing my scarf.

"There," Transformer says.
"But I can't reach the strings."
"Perfect."

FASCIST

I want to learn the harmonica. For a change. To rest my fingers. Until the blisters heal. But Transformer won't like it.
That machine puts people to sleep.

MENTOR

She's heard enough. From downstairs, she appears to herald the future of rock 'n' roll.

"You need lessons."

Lessons. Lessons from a mentor.

"That's mental," Transformer says. But Flowers is adamant. This punk kid from the bird streets is the chosen one. Her brother runs Brian's Music Store at the shopping centre, where Flowers bought our guitars in the first place. His name isn't even Brian. His name is Paul.

"Mentor? More like tormentor," says Transformer.

"Shush, you."

"Duh, have you heard her solo?"

I have. Not Flowers. The kid is pro. Once when we went to buy strings at the shopping centre, she was inside the store trying out an amp. While Transformer waited to pay, I got to watch her strangle a red Telecaster. She flicked the pickups and played Etch-A-Sketch harmonics high up the neck. Then she ditched the Telecaster and turned around and grabbed a Les Paul off the rack, held it up behind her head and played it blind. Dressed in tartan and wearing combat boots, she soloed "Purple Haze" by Jimi Hendrix.

"Let's go," Transformer said when he came to get me. He couldn't even look at her.

Hendrix though. A dead giveaway that underneath the dress code she wasn't that different from any kid with absent parents raised on a subscription to *Guitar Magazine*.

BIRDS

Starling. Robin. Swallow. Thrush. The bird streets have no sidewalks. As streets go, the birds are introverted, short, and kind of useless. They twist and turn. They lead nowhere. Not long ago, I was on the bus with Flowers going through the birds when she pointed at the houses out the window.

"Those are all rentals."

Like it was a big deal. Rentals. I couldn't really see why. Spit lives on Robin, where I saw lots of kids running between houses playing tag. It seemed like they were having goofy fun. Anyway, the neighbourhood does remind me of a campground. Small lots with a temporary feel.

NUISANCE

We live on the far side of Strathmore and the birds, between the highway and the lake and close enough to the airport to get the jets coming in low.

Somehow our house stands right at the Stop sign midway down the street, at 305 Sources.

"A real nuisance" is often how Flowers describes the parade of cars that come rolling to a stop at the end of our driveway, as if to pay respects. But to whom? To my grandparents from Sweden is the best answer. Who else but Mormor and Morfar? Who, despite having more than a decade of Canada under their belts, are arranged like foreign dignitaries in lawn chairs every weekday afternoon behind the cedars that separate the yard from the intersection. Flowers and sometimes my sister Candy join them out on the lawn for coffee and cake. The cars passing on the other side of the hedge impose on their afternoon peace summit. The presence of intruders disrupts this particular idyll: Morfar in his white golf cap, the newspaper opened on his knee. Mormor seated beside him, face upturned, eyes closed, the top buttons of her blouse undone to take sun. And Flowers herself, who is next in line to the crown, up to taking her share of sun.

"Taking their clothes off" is what Candy calls it. "What kind of example does it set?"

"Oh, you," Flowers will say to that, "don't be a nuisance too," insinuating again that Candy is being a pain just like the slowpoke drivers who idle behind the cedars only to encroach on the Swedes' peaceful summit of sunshine and coffee and cake.

I observe this all from the roof while smoking a ciggy as Transformer and I are taking a well-earned break from our travails. From up here, I can see the treetops rising above the bird streets and Uncle Per's car arriving late. For real, Candy accepts that taking sun with black coffee is part of the little Europe we inhabit at 305 Sources. What other traditions do we have? None. Except for drinking Aquavit and singing Swedish songs at Christmas and on New Year's Eve. Our family has been taking sun from behind the cedars ever since I can remember, perhaps to store it up and smuggle it back to the North Country one day.

ARCHIPELAGOS

First lesson on a Sunday afternoon. She tells us what we already know: that her name is Spit, and that since we're beginners, she'll go easy on us.

"Just be civilized," says Transformer.

Three new chords and a major scale. Beginner stuff. As lead strummer of the band, my job is to learn some chords while Transformer gets lost in the notes of the archipelagos.

"They're called arpeggios."

"Spell it."

She hesitates.

It will be a lesson for her as well.

"How long have you been playing?"

"Ages."

She smirks and unpacks her own guitar, a semi-hollow spaceship moulded from old-fashioned cherry. A sci-fi antique.

"It's a Gretsch," she says. We both gasp. *A Gretzky?* Hell, it must be handy to have an older brother who works in a music store.

"Our mothers are clerks at the same bank," she announces, making revelatory small talk. I steal a glance at Transformer. *Nothing.* "My mom was there first. We came over when I was six."

"The British Invasion, eh?" Him of the archipelagos.

"Not really." She glances up at the Borg poster over his headboard. Borg with the headband and Donnay racket. With the Tarzan figure and ice-blue eyes. Our private Viking. Our Lord of the Rings. "Obviously, I don't have an accent anymore. I've been to three different schools. We move around a lot. I skipped a grade. I'm usually the shrimp of my class. I used to do things like suck on my bangs…"

Transformer's not saying anything, so I'm not. The fact is we have never had a visitor to our room that talked this much. "I used to have long hair. It was unsanitary. I had bad acne too. I was gross."

"What school do you go to now?" I say, to stop the history lesson.

"John 23rd."

Never heard of it.

"It's Catholic."

Still never heard of it.

"I'm Catholic."

Adds up.

"What are you?"

She's doing the talking, and meanwhile Transformer has gone to the roof for a ciggy break. *What about us? What are we?* Once I asked Flowers that very question and she stared at me with such an expression, as though she had never been told of my existence.

"That sounds weird," I say.

"Not to me." She's deadpan. "So where do you go to school?"

She is talking to me and observing Transformer.

"I go to Bethune."

"Bethune?"

Named after Norman Bethune.

"It's a private school in Dollard."

"Fancy. Can you afford that?"

What a question. I've never thought about it. I don't even get good grades.

"What about him?"

Him is picking at a scab on his knee, now flicking a penknife at the strawberry. Him doesn't attend fancy Bethune. Not anymore. There is a story behind that. I wish I knew what it was.

"He's going to New School. Starting next year."

"New School?"

I try for the monkey's attention: "Want to tell Spit about New School, Transformer?"

"You tell her…" comes the answer, although the monkey climbs back in through the window to explain the following: "You're allowed to take tons of spares at this school, and we can graduate from grade eleven without learning that cell sex is called mitosis."

"Impressive." She snorts. Her nostrils flare, which I like. "I'm pretty sure that I'll graduate from the John without hearing the word."

"Tough," Transformer says.

Changing the subject, I ask our mentor: "Hey, what's your real name?"

"I forget."

Funny.

Transformer, posing for the mirror, unplugged, is playing high up the neck of his guitar, his finger work emitting the whine of a mosquito.

"Originally, he took the name Zimbra for himself."

Transformer beats his chest: "...*bimba* ... *I zimbra*."

"You like Talking Heads?"

Who doesn't?

"*Gadji beri bimba...*" he goes.

"But so your mother said you were starting a punk band." Spit looks around our room a bit. "What records do you have?"

The records are in a pile under the desk. "We're getting more," Transformer blurts, returning to standard English, very worried that I will spill the beans about our origins, retrace the family DNA to ABBA, reveal attachment issues to Elton John. But he can relax. Of all records, his new favourite Lou Reed is the one showing.

VICIOUS

I jump to the mirror after she leaves.

"She's vicious! Vicious! Vicious! She's vicious! Vicious! She's so vicious!"

"Cool it," Transformer grimaces. "Anyway, that's not it. Give it to me."

"No."

It's my guitar.

"Don't be a baby."

Feeding the hand that teases me, I ease the strap off my shoulder.

"Ready for this?" Holding my left-handed guitar upside down, Transformer puts himself front and centre before the mirror. And takes it from the top.

"Vicious. Vicious! She's so vicious! Vicious! Vicious! She's vicious! Vicious! She's so vicious! Vicious! She's so vicious! Vicious! Vicious! She's vicious! Vicious! She's vicious!"

Turns to face. "That's how it's done."

What's the difference?

The music dies and the needle lifts, and for our next treat he selects a live album called *One for the Road*, its glossy front cover all hot pink and yellow, with this bow-tied guitarist looking puckered and sassy. After playing it on repeat yesterday, it's become a house favourite. Transformer places it down on the turntable's platter using two hands to plant the bomb, and then he races back into bed and gets ready to listen.

There's static, some pop before the spacey organ and guitar intro takes over.

Then that voice.

"Ray!"

"Ray Davies!"

Ray and his brother Dave, the lead guitarist of the Kinks, get into fistfights on stage. All the time!

"From Muswell Hill!"

Credit *Hit Parader*, a monthly music magazine Transformer will journey to the mall and back for by bus, for this esoteric knowledge about the origins of the Kinks. The magazine is super jam-packed with photographs, and the cover features lots of glam-rock singers and heavy-metal guitarists. The headshots of these sweaty monsters are scary. Once a month, a new one stares out at us convict-style from inside the penitentiary of rock like addiction waiting to happen.

"The borough of Muswell Hill."

Transformer is strangling the blanket, killing himself laughing.

"Muswell Hill! It sounds like a playground made for mice… for toy mice!"

I happen to agree with him on this. Muswell Hill sounds a lot like a borough invented for that very purpose, as a playground for mice in London Town.

"Ray!"

How we love the charm of Ray Davies. We could listen to Ray croon all afternoon, pass the day on Hollywood Boulevard, and follow this charming man as he meanders through a fabled place where everybody's a star, and everybody's in movies… but we have lots of band work to do. For one thing, we have Uncle Per's roots garbage to weed through. Transformer is adamant we do something about our roots before Spit gets a closer look at our collection. He slips the edition of *Hit Parader* under his pillow for another time.

"Let's start," Transformer says and nods for me to drag into view the scandalous milk crate containing our inheritance. Transformer sits himself at the desk, in position to do the deed. He is ready like an accountant to flip through the filthy lucre, record after record, and for the next three hours, about the only thing we say to each other is:

"Put something else on."

Canned Heat.

"Put something else on."

CSNY.

"Put something else on."

The Byrds.

"Put something else on."

T Rex.

"Put something else on."

Janis Joplin.

"Put something else on."

Moody Blues.

Manfred Mann.

Ten Years After.

"Something else."

Emerson, Lake & Palmer.

"Something else!"

The Mamas & the Papas.

"Who?"

Procol Harum.

"What?"

Television.

"Stop—keep it."

Marquee Moon sticks.

"Put it on again."

Estranged, taut guitars.

"Again!"

Deranged lead vocals.

"One more time!"

Television has at least two amazing players on the guitar. I could never do this kind of music. I don't have the hands.

"You don't have to worry." Transformer reads my mind. "We're doing our stuff."

That's a relief. I can do our stuff.

LEPRECHAUNS

Spit gives us the U2 single "I Will Follow" as a present. She says she has two copies. We need it for today's lesson: we are to learn a new technique, the harmonic strumming invented by the Edge.

"The *wha*—?" Transformer stammers.

"Smarten up." She unclips the latches of her guitar case. Glances at the Expos pennant on my side of the room. "All the best bands are from Ireland."

"Big deal." Transformer is nonplussed. "So are leprechauns."

"What's he talking about?"

"Nothing," I say absently while beholding the seven-inch single by U2 and combing its gasoline sheen for clues. "Where did you hear this?"

"Not on fake-music radio." Spit sounds utterly disgusted. She means FM. "I went down to Dutchy's."

Dutchy's Record Cave is a downtown store. I don't get to go there without a chaperon. Transformer might take me someday.

"Dutchy's is a good place." She's directing her speech solely at me though Transformer's in the room too. She can do that. "Have you been to Rock en Stock? Dutchy's and

Rock en Stock are cool unless you're looking for bootlegs. For bootlegs, go to Phantasmagoria." Spit's not making this up. Phantasmagoria, Dutchy's, Rock en Stock—that's Montreal's holy trinity of record shops right there. Bootlegs are a big deal. The word makes me laugh. *Bootleg*. It must be invented. Bootlegs are illegal. We don't have any. Even if the sound is usually muddy, you can pay a lot for a live bootleg that's been recorded by some pirate hiding underneath the main stage at Budokan.

"If you're a collector," she goes, "check out Phantasmagoria," slowly lifting the Gretsch from the velvet crypt. "I've got a forty-minute live recording of 'Kashmir.' It takes up two sides of the record."

"That's a waste," Transformer says, "of both sides."

She lets it go: his commentary, his demeanour, his Transformerness is the price of admission, and Flowers is paying her good money to stay put and mentor us together. Before she's done tuning, Transformer's up at the mirror striking poses again, shadow-boxing the punk rocker within, while I'm stuck staring at her, spellbound as Spit brings the semi-hollow to her stomach and sets it there on top of her knees and then leans toward the amp and plugs in.

"Let me show you something," she says, and we're back to the Edge. Transformer drops to the bed and slumps against the wall. *This is going to be a drag.* I maintain my front-row seat, my feet dangling from the desk before that beautiful guitar as Spit proceeds to strum, making a rapid motion first. She steps on the delay box and gets it going—the effect, a fluttering sound—her vibrating palm hanging in a blur like a hummingbird over the strings.

Abruptly she stops.

"You try."

It's magic.

Him first. Transformer's all clunky, wrist moving slow like he's mixing cement. Then it's my turn.

"Use this guitar," Spit says.

"I'm left-handed."

"Poor you," she says and steps on the delay pedal. "Once you get the technique, it's easy."

"Shit."

I'm impressed.

The thing is Spit can play better than us, but she doesn't write songs. She's what Transformer calls a technician. A technician is someone who practises a lot and knows their instrument inside out. Basically, a technician is a musician. Technicians control what they do. Whereas we don't, not really.

"We're like idiot savants," Transformer announced to me earlier this week.

"No, we're not."

"Trust me."

"Why?"

"Because you're my little brother."

Because. Just fucking because.

A technician like Spit is all scales and suspended fifths and covers. Maybe technicians respect music too much to want to make their own, or something like that. On the other hand, I have never wanted to learn *anyone's* song, and still I hardly know how to play. Learn covers? Not interested. Transformer is the same. Maybe that's what Transformer means about us being idiots.

HOMBRE

I get this crap Ibanez. It has a sunburst front like a Strat but when plugged in sounds like a tin can dragging on a dirt road behind a jalopy. Whatever a jalopy is.

"You sound shit, Hombre."

Hombre. Transformer has a new name for me.

"Don't call me that."

"Why not? You're playing a Spanish guitar."

Transformer makes us all in his image. Like a god, like a fascist. Mom is Flowers because she's the gardener and because in a photograph of her and my father in San Francisco—the one she keeps on her bedside table—she's basically wearing a hippie sundress. Our sister is Candy or Sister Candy for no good reason. Her real name is Catherine. The Swedes are the power trio of taking sun fame, Flowers' parents Mormor and Morfar. Since he discovered disco, Uncle Per is sometimes referred to as Sparky. Sparky from the vomit side.

I flip the Ibanez in my lap to display the manufacturer's label. "MADE IN USA. Says right here."

"So?"

"It's not a Spanish guitar."

"How about Panny then, Mr. Panny?"

Yes, Mr. Panny is our man, he's so full of gasoline that he's always, always clean!

"You scared?"

We're just teasing you, Mr. Panny.

Transformer drags his claw through his hair. "You're in a band, so who do you want to be?"

He took his name from Lou Reed.

"I don't know yet."

For now, I'm Hombre.

STAY

In the evening, Transformer sits himself on the window ledge, guitar in lap. Fits there, leg dangling, one knee cocked against the frame. He's loaded, a compressed spring.

"Hombre, let's write a song using these…" Transformer says, grappling with new chords and the finger positions that must cramp his hand.

I'm down on the floor strumming the new chords and realizing they don't sound like anything I've heard before. Neither majors nor minors. Orphans, they must be. Suspended fifths or sevenths? I don't have a clue. We don't read music, which means we're flying blind from accident to accident. I don't mind it. Who wants to *read* music? After each lesson, we end up with a bunch of messed-up fingerings that no one else in the music universe knows about.

"Sure, these sound really good." Put through my purple chorus pedal, the chords gurgle from the amplifier as if from under water.

The chords are wet, the progression is dripping.

"There's a song here, we're getting close," says Transformer from the windowsill, his own idle guitar sleeping across his lap. "Just keep going. We'll find it. Keep playing, keep going, just keep going, keep going."

It's dark out. Usually when Transformer gets going, he squirms facing the closet mirror, muscular like a cobra, following his own movements as he tries to make the other him blink first. Tonight, he's acting different. No mirror and no alter-cobra. He's taken by something and won't move from his perch on the window ledge. He's staying put and close to the cool night air, the trees and the mass of shadows and the sprinklers working like crickets.

"Keep going… a bit further. Don't stop."

But now I must stop, if only to adjust my position, and the last chord I play resonates as reverb and delay wash out of the amp and the waves of my orphan fingerings foam like breakers when they hit the walls across the room. Alas, I start up again after moving onto the bed, but right away Transformer interrupts me. "Tune up. Tune up again, Hombre."

When Spit orders Transformer to tune, it bothers him because tuning is more difficult than playing a song like U2's "I Will Follow," which is all adrenaline and down-strumming high up the neck on two shitty-bitty chords. Tuning is a procedure. Tuning is technician-level stuff. Transformer has a bit of an ear for it, but my receivers are junk for this kind of thing. While I begin my fiddling around, tightening, loosening strings, Transformer grows impatient—"Hurry up!"—finally slapping his foot against the window frame. "That's good enough!"

Fine. But it's my turn to set the scene. "This time, I'm going to play the same thing but play it differently."

"Genius." Transformer laughs for once.

"I mean it."

"Just start."

Beginnings are important. I strum softly and build slowly and Transformer mumbles, hums, and sniffs out the sweet spot. Sways his dangling foot while I keep it steady, the best I can.

From this room, I can see the world
Blue and green, and black at night

His voice startles me.

From this time, I am going away
In this world, I cannot stay

"From This Room," July 1981. For the record, it's our new best song.

DARNED

Eventually we learn Montreal has its own music scene, and we are not in it. We are far from it, in Dorval. It was staring us in our small faces, if only we'd taken a moment before now to read the newspaper we deliver on Thursdays.

Transformer is transfixed, lying on his stomach. Half off the bed. Poking through the local music listings.

"Wait for me." I shove over beside him. The newspaper is spread out on the floor beneath our low altitude. He reads aloud.

"Ray Condo and the Hard Rock Goners play Saturday at Le Terrace. Deja Voodoo on the same bill. Condition at Tattoo. Sons of the Desert… Jah Cutta… Kali & Dub Inc.… Disappointed a Few People. American Devices. The Snitches. Weather Permitting… The Darned."

"Who?"

"D-A-R-N-E-D. Get it?"

"I'm not stupid."

But I don't get it.

"The Darned at Station 10 on Friday night." He's found a review. Transformer narrates: "The Darned is a four-piece cow-punk band that leans more art than anger. The lead singer has the mouth of a poet. Her friendly eyes belie a serial killer's grin. The three-man back-up band is spare. No bombast huddled there. The drummer is squeaky clean. The bass player is no fuss. The guitarist is good nature incarnate with a taste for taut barbed-wire-solos and won't play a ragged note out of place."

"They sound good," I say.

"The usual bullshit review." Transformer's not impressed. "Plus, have a look. This reviewer is about twelve years old."

There's only a headshot of Megan Lynch, the music reporter with dark hair and freckles.

"She might just have a young face," I say.

"And what is that?" Honestly, Transformer should know. Flowers remarks on the young faces of complete strangers all the time. *That gentleman has a young face. Doesn't he?* I've started to notice this phenomenon even with familiar faces like that of our neighbour Mrs. Willey. Mrs. Willey has an oddly young face. Even Uncle Per.

However, Transformer's sour face is not buying it.

"There's no such thing, Hombre." Extra copies of the *Chronicle* pile up in our room. Once a month, we go out collecting door to door. And sometimes get invited inside to the most sad and smelly rooms of the neighbourhood. Nobody on our route has a young face. "I bet Megan is a student. They rob the cradle. The *Chronicle* isn't even a real newspaper," Transformer continues, making his case. "The real newspaper man in town to impress is Lepage from *The Gazette*. That man hates everything."

Lepage. French name, but he's English. Candy went to

the same high school as Lepage. Dorval High. Lepage put the high in that school. That's how we know him. From Candy, who describes him as very shy. He wears tiny wire–rimmed glasses and he will blink you to death, she says. Apparently, he still goes around in the same jean jacket he got in grade eight. But he's the real thing, a reporter for the city paper.

"Don't be fooled by his demeanour, he's knife sharp," Transformer cautions me.

With the listings laid out on the floor, I'm more interested in the photo of Megan than by Transformer's running commentary on Lepage.

"He has powers. A full article every Saturday. Lepage can decide our fate with a single review." A review of what though? We don't perform. We have no recordings. We barely exist.

"Stop staring at her, Hombre. Give it back to me. Are you blushing?"

I'm not, but I am. So I immediately surrender Megan's young face without having had the time I wanted. Even so, she is hard to forget. Transformer resumes his roll-calling of names.

"Terminal Sunglasses. Global Village Idiots. This Blue Piano. Bare Bones. Secret Act. The Gruesomes. Seven Sisters. Three O' Clock Train. The Mongols. The Asexuals. Vomit and the Zits. The Local Rabbits."

"Vomit and the Zits?"

"Jealous?"

"No."

"Now pay attention and listen to our name: Because."

"I'm familiar with it."

He repeats it. "Because."

"So?"

"Because sounds seventies. It could be from the sixties. Because is square."

I don't say anything, just fucking because naming the band Because was mostly my idea. And because Transformer's running full of gas.

"In the beginning was Because, and the name Because was not a good idea because it's for babies."

But *he's* the baby.

"We're behind the times, Hombre. Out of sync."

"Are we breaking up?"

"Nah. Maybe some fresh blood, that's all."

A human sacrifice?

"Listen. Jealousy, love, and hate are the ghost in sibling rivalries. We're part of some great pattern. Rock 'n' roll repeats the same conceits. Get it?"

Kind of. I get that someday we're going to fight the worst feelings about each other. I foresee us playing live and screaming murder. Performing live as a band is going to be life-threatening. The songs will deliver our confused SOS to a scene we are afraid of. Nobody out there is signed to a record label. Nobody we know. Still. Signed is shorthand for getting neutered. I know that. Signed is for Supertramp and Styx, for old-school braggarts and pricks. Signed is selling out. Getting signed is what everybody must secretly want? I comprehend that a few truths are self-evident: the labels are out to swindle the little nobodies, the majors are sweet honey for sucks, and getting yourself signed is tantamount to treason against post-punk DIY. There is occasionally friction between Transformer and me, but it's early days, without the spectre of onstage fisticuffs or any reason for legal battles about copyright playing out in the press. I get all this stuff about labels and the scene and about being the brothers in a band.

"What usually happens is the alpha sibling begins to hog the limelight while his nondescript brother slips inside the Bermuda Triangle of the rhythm section, never to be seen or heard from again until a lousy solo effort ten to fifteen years later."

He's laughing about it. But I also understand that Transformer and I "get" each other in a way that defies a lot of bullshit. We have the type of connection thousands of people must search for their entire lives, and we've found it, right here, in this room.

Don't ask me how.

DEAD LISTENER

Spit, I am doing as promised and addressing this as per your instructions, c/o South Pole, Antarctica.

This was your idea. I'd been an orderly for years already before you made a guest appearance on the ward. I was a hospital vet, you could say, but in all that time had never adapted to the deserted feel of the wards in the evening after the end of family visiting hours. To get through the night shift, I hid in the utility room watching muted TV. If the call bell sounded, it could mean only one of two things. Some poor soul hadn't made it to the toilet; or some soul, some unique soul, had died. Either way, there was a body to wash.

Fancy finding you sitting upright in a side-rail adjustable bed.

"You're a conehead too," you chirped, altogether nonplussed, as though you had been expecting me to come along in surgery greens that fit like pyjamas.

"I guess."

"Seriously, you're a skinhead now?"

"Not even close." We resorted to banter. It had the desired effect of pretending everything was normal. But it was anything but ordinary.

"When did this start happening?"

"A while ago."

"Well," smiling. "Finally, you look punk."

"Touché."

"I'm serious. I'll still be your groupie, Hombre."

"Very funny."

"Well, that's how it was." Pulling knees up, leaning forward. "Even if you were freaks."

"I'm still doing my part."

"I'm sure you are. Wow. Hombre."

"In the flesh."

"Anyone in your life?"

"I'm a loner."

"'Loneliness is holiness.'"

"That's right."

"Isn't that from one of your songs?"

You spoke of yesterday like it was today. Yesterday was bedrock.

"You were lucky that your grandparents lived in the same house with you."

"They just did," I said.

You tapped on your kneecaps. "Remember the time your grandmother came in when we were jamming? And your grandfather, he was a real gentleman."

He still is, still is.

Sitting in the bed and wearing a black hoodie, fists locked in a kangaroo pouch, you resembled a hooded monk, a sunken spirit.

"What about you?" I had to ask.

"You mean all this?" Gesturing palms up. "My room with a view?" You rubbed the IV in your arm absently, fingernails clawing the hypoallergenic tape. "It's better than Halifax, I can say that. Halifax wasn't any fun. Neither was high school. I never fit in. I guess I never fit in anywhere. We returned here for treatment, so I could be salvaged. Montreal is great."

"I'm sorry."

"Don't be. You know what they say: there's no time to be sorry about the things we can't change."

"How long have you been in here?"

"A while. I had the radioactive iodine treatment last week. Can you see? Am I still glowing?"

"No."

"I do in the dark. Hey, change of subject: you better be still playing that Ibanez, Signor. I gave up guitar too early. That's one thing I regret. I sold my stuff. I hope you haven't. Paul's studio is still doing well. You should record with him. Really."

Irony, and tiptoeing around.

"You're a lot more serious than I remember, Hombre. Wow. It's hard to imagine you as anything other than that kid. But so, you're not tempted, not busking?"

"I don't have the presence." I didn't back then.

"You have plenty. I'm the one with the disappearing act."

"Don't say that."

"Well, it's true."

"Is there anything I can do?"

"You can take my tray away to start with."

"Nothing else you need?"

What a stupid question.

"Drugs."

Truthfully, a good answer.

"Wait. Maybe I do have something for you, a special mission. You can get me out of here. Don't worry. It's above board. Paul's done it. There's somewhere I want to go with you."

GETTING A GIG

PULL

There's no time to change our boring name. Our first gig could be in a few weeks!

Where?

In the dayroom on the sixth floor of the Veterans' Hospital in Sainte-Anne-de-Bellevue, where the sun goes down on the world wars.

Why there?

Because we're fuckin' nobodies, that's why.

Because Sister Candy, a nurse's aide, has some pull with the Vets.

"How long a set?"

"Oh, it doesn't really matter," Candy says, adjusting the towel underneath her. Flowers and the Swedes are settled in the lawn chairs while Sister Candy has found her separate peace, sunbathing to the American Top 40. Her AM radio whispers are static from my height.

"It does matter."

"Let's go back in," Transformer says. "We're wasting our time out here. It's too hot. We need to rehearse."

"I wouldn't worry about it," Candy says, glancing at Flowers. "Just do what you would normally do."

"That sounds like the best advice," Flowers says without acknowledging we normally don't *do* anything.

Transformer puts a finger gun to the side of his head.

"Now, would you boys like to come down for coffee and a piece of *kladdkaka*?"

The Swedes say "kaka" for cake. Imagine the revolution over there: "Let them eat kaka!"

"Not me, thank you," I say. "We have to practise."

"Before you go, say hello to Far."

Transformer steps to the ledge. "Hello Fart."

That's an old one.

Morfar lifts his gaze. "Ja, hello boys."

Mormor catches the drift in Swedish: "Va saya du?"

Flowers grimaces, gives Transformer a stern look. Him is trouble.

Back to the setting of the gig, and Candy says, "It won't be your big break or anything, but everybody needs to start somewhere, right?"

"She's, like, our manager now?" Transformer grumbles into his armpit.

Meanwhile, a rattle at the side gate. Enter Sparky wearing the white jumpsuit. He gives Mormor a peck on the cheek, then takes a seat and shields his eyes with a salute to block the sun.

"What's this about a show? Are you playing the Mapes?"

Mapes is shorthand for the Maples Inn, a hippie slum in Pointe Claire. The Edgewater and the Green Hornet are some other places around here. The paper route takes us west along the lakeshore, past the Green Hornet to the apartment buildings in Valois Bay. The Green Hornet has a boxing ring and scheduled fights. No big names like Roberto Durán, who defeated Sugar Ray Leonard for the welterweight championship. That brawl went down last summer at the Olympic Stadium, not at a place like the Green Hornet. Still sometimes in the empty parking lot, sparked by the old marquee, small kids duke it out. Rhyme to the music of this time and place. The Edge is a disco further along. Transformer and I have never set foot in any of these places. Wouldn't if you kicked us in the head or bribed us.

"Just joking," Sparky rescues himself. "I heard you're

playing the Vets. Need a drive?"

"Like we need a roadie." Transformer mangles it softly.

"Up to you." Sparky tinkles the cup and saucer resting in his lap.

"The cheque is in the mail." Transformer edges further down the roof.

"Don't get so close," Flowers says.

He ignores her and moves closer to the ledge.

"Hold on to the ladder," Flowers says.

"Don't be an idiot," Candy says.

Everybody is watching now as he manoeuvres and turns and squats so his back is facing the fall and his eyes are on me. It comes naturally to him. Being the centre of attention, the eye of the storm. It's something he perfected last summer at the Drown Right Away. We'd ride over to the pool with the Willey twins and some kids from down the street and around the corner, the gang of us timing it to show up ten minutes before free swim. We'd lock our bikes outside the chalet and shower inside before stepping straight onto the bright concrete surrounding the swimming pool. Free swim lasts but one hour. The lifeguard whistles. Then it's time for everybody to scramble out of the water and stand dripping in a ring along the edge while a second lifeguard dives into the water with a line of bobs and closes off the deep end. After that, the lifeguard on the chair blows again, and the shallow end is reopened for business, and anybody who wants to practise their dives lines up behind the board. What a sight that is: seven or eight excited boys and girls blowing into cupped hands, ribs thrashing on the skinny kids. Performing a dive off the end of the board is always a big deal. It requires a moment of courage. To do the cannon-ball, the jackknife, belly flop, forward run-and-flip. My act is to walk off the end of the board without breaking stride. Something too simple for words, yet I never accomplish it without flinching from the inside out. Transformer's thing is the scuba roll. He walks straight out to the end of the board, turns around to crouch, knees tucked, and wills himself to capsize.

I've tried that a couple of times but can't bring myself to fall backwards. Not many people can. But Transformer, he can.

"Come on, Transformer," I call to him. "Stop it."

He wags his tongue at me.

"I mean it."

"Hold the ladder," Flowers urges him.

"Grow up," Candy says.

"I'm trying," he says, and at last he stands vertical and walks up the slant of the roof towards where I'm crouched by the wall.

"So…" My line of questioning about the gig is about to resume. I'm worried about the basics. "You're sure we can bring an amplifier?"

"I don't see a problem," Candy says.

"You must be the big boss over there, eh?"

More noise than signal, Candy disregards Transformer.

"Your amplifier is tiny. These are vets, Hombre. Men of war. They've been in the trenches. They experienced more deafening explosions than Transformer's guitar."

"Which war?" I'm suddenly curious.

"Korea. World Wars I and II."

"*All* of them?"

"No, stupid." Candy says. "Nobody was in all of them. That would be impossible."

On cue, Sparky begins reeling off dates: "Korea was 1950 to 1954. World War II 1939 to 1945. Hitler, Churchill, Stalin, Eisenhower." Sparky is a history buff. He's talking for my benefit. The rest tune him out. Shutter their eyes. Take shelter. "The Great War was 1914 to 1918. The first flame-thrower… mustard gas… the Great War changed humanity fundamentally."

Transformer yawns. He's taken more than enough friendly fire. He stands. Overlooking little Europe, he begins reciting poetry for my sake.

"*We are dead. Short days ago, we lived, felt dawn, saw sunset glow, loved and were loved…*" His voice trails off. In a whisper meant for only me, he resumes: "John McCrae. A war poet. You'll be reading him next year in English. McCrae, Trotter, and the other plodders. Talk to Dawson. He's got something to say about the war poets. Lots to say about everything."

Transformer means Mr. Dawson, the guidance counsellor at Bethune. I haven't met him yet. But in the fall, I will.

Wiping hands free of pellets, Transformer comes back around to the gig. "We'll have to play two sets. Definitely."

"Better get moving, Hombre," says Candy, who grasps our band dynamics. As Transformer's dedicated rhythm slave, I'll need to write some new songs quick to keep the peace. Not that I have any control over the process. Some days, honey drips from the strings. My guitar sings, and around we go. Other days, my fingertips are so raw I can barely strum.

Candy turns onto her back and rests on her elbows. She eyes us both. "It wouldn't hurt if you sprinkled in a few covers."

"Like what? Beethoven's Ninth? 'Waterloo'?" Transformer is mortified.

"If you had a manager, you wouldn't make such a fuss about playing covers. Your manager would *make* you."

"Managers are dicks."

"Watch your language." Flowers comes to life.

"Come on, Transformer. Lighten up," Sparky says, joining the conversation. "Why not learn some catchy song from my old records?"

"And sell out? Spend all our inheritance at once?"

"What inheritance?" Flowers asks.

"Learn a couple. It's not a big deal."

"Covers are for cocks."

"Watch your language." Again Flowers.

"You'll never make any money," Candy concludes. "'Fuck Creation' is a great song but it's not going to pay the bills. I'm sorry. That's the truth."

"Let's move." Transformer knocks me on the shoulder. "Forget this crowd. We'll take our chances."

COVERS

Covers are for cocks. Does it bear repeating? Transformer believes in what he's talking about, often without knowing what he's talking about. With ardour. That's the thing about Transformer. But we're on the same wavelength here: playing covers is for loser cocks. What's the use of playing other people's music? It's not for us to please what he calls the madding crowd. Being in a tribute band is about the saddest thing on earth I can imagine. It would be like being a young painter and, at your vernissage, instead of hanging your own paintings, you go and tear a bunch of pages from a Disney colouring book and stick them on the wall.

BAYONETS

Word on the street is Because need to write at least five more songs to play a complete set.

Fast-forward to the hospital sunroom and a platoon of angry vets jabbing bayonets into the air, hollering, "*Encore!*"

Bethune is the only private school in the district. On this part of the island of Montreal, there's no old money. There's just new money. New money doesn't have the same value, but you can buy the same things with it. I overheard Uncle Per saying something about this once. He was talking to Flowers about sending me to Bethune.

Though tuition is steep, Bethune has no tradition. "No pedigree," Transformer says. "To compensate, the administration invented this uniform." Dressed in my green blazer, grey slacks, white shirt, tie. "This insubstantial pageant." He spins around before the mirror. "Hombre. Here's to the harder stuff Because are made of."

Sure. His stolen soliloquy is the old stuff of last year, from the final months of his private school tenure, when Transformer liked to mock Bethune for adopting a pseudo-paramilitary class system of prefects. Well, guess what? Before school was let out in June, the administration made me one of four junior prefects.

"Tell them you're in a band," Transformer says, playing hangman with the school tie. "Warn them you're going punk. Go ahead and tell Mr. Principal that over the summer you incubated tons and wrote a pretty little thing called

'Fuck Creation.'"

"That won't work."

It won't. Anointed as I shall be before the entire student body at morning assembly, being selected for prefect duty is cruel: on the first Monday morning of the year, it qualifies as school-assisted suicide. It's the perfect crime against popularity. During the lunch hour, I'm supposed to supervise games in the parking lot. Fun.

"Then talk to Mr. Dawson. He might help you."

I'm dying to meet the famed Mr. Dawson. And sooner or later, I will. But for now, I dread school. I fear for my life. Plus, on top of everything, I worry about the gig and having to perform a set of songs that don't exist.

Some days, becoming a junior prefect seems like the easy route out.

VOW

Meanwhile, Transformer proclaims that he's *seriously considering* a vow of silence. Him. Taking a vow of silence. Why? For what?

"Like a hunger strike."

"You can't *announce* it," I say. "Especially not now. You can't just announce that you're going to take a vow of silence."

"Shut up, Hombre."

"You can't—"

"Quit your lawyer bollocks. While I'm still thinking about it, I can."

"That makes no sense."

"Ours is the age of accepting what doesn't make sense."

"And who said that?"

Probably Mr. Dawson. Probably he whispered this in Transformer's ear last year. For ours is the age of eating a lot of shit.

"It doesn't matter. Everything's worth nothing. Trust me, you can't escape the rat race unless you starve yourself or something. It's all a big-time swindle. Don't you get it?"

Not really.

"Brute silence is a choice."

Is it?

"The only choice."

The next many seconds are aborted by brute silence.

Finally, I ask, "What will Flowers do if she finds out?"

"I'm not telling Flowers."

But word will get out.

"How about Candy?"

"She'll applaud like a seal."

"That's Candy."

"Sister Candy, the nun."

"What?"

"Never mind."

Transformer slashes at his guitar. Time to make some noise. He picks away at some new chords and expects me to follow. When I refuse to go along, he gets offended.

"What's wrong now?"

He's irritated with me, as if I'm the one now talking about taking a vow of silence.

"The plane," I say, nodding upwards. Transformer is a beat late but catches on. When the jets come in from the direction of the lake, landing gear a pair of claws hanging from the belly, we usually freeze up and stop living. That's when we're safe inside. Getting caught on the roof under the roar spells annihilation. Transformer is usually the first to catch on, almost as though he has built-in radar or an early-warning system. He told me once that he got itchy, prickly for incoming. Not this time. Thunder envelops our mood. It stretches, erases, then releases us twenty seconds later. We come out somewhere else.

"Can I ask a question?"

Transformer rolls his eyes as the thunder melts towards the airport.

"What?"

"Can you tell me what you're going to think about—I mean, after you take your vow?"

"How do I know? I'm not getting married."

"What?"

"Why don't you go ask Morfar instead of me? He doesn't talk much. Does he?"

No, he doesn't. Except on formal occasions like on New Year's Eve, which is also his birthday. None of the house Swedes is a big talker. Sparky doesn't count. Morfar is a gentleman. He's quiet but he will do anything to help people. He goes shopping when Flowers is at the bank, and he joins the neighbours to shovel snow in the winter. When he was a boy of thirteen in Gothenburg, he ran away from home. He made it as far as the railway tracks, where he opened a pack of cigarettes and smoked one after the other until he vomited. He left home for good when he turned sixteen. I was told this by Flowers. The fact he ran away from home seemed to make her proud and sad at the same time. The fact that she's talking about events that happened in Sweden a long time ago makes me feel a bit strange, especially now when I look at him as an old man.

"And for your information, it's not like I'll be trying to solve a math problem. I'm not doing it just to be able to raise my hand afterwards and say something clever. Anyway, nobody can speak to the important things."

"I guess." I study my own hands.

"See what I mean."

No.

"Forget it."

Just one last question: "What about the band? And our gig. You're still going to sing a few songs? Right?"

"The band is different. I told you that."

He didn't. But that's a relief.

GUIDANCE

I'm finally having my first meeting with Mr. Dawson. It takes place inside a windowless office that shares a cinder block wall with the gymnasium. The rendezvous nature of it all is unnerving enough without the hollow boom resounding each time a soccer ball smacks the other side of the wall.

"Think of that noise as your subconscious," Dawson says. "It probably has something to say and wants in on our conversation."

Fine, but it's distracting. Most students see him as a double agent, as a fink doing their parents' dirty work on the inside. My connection is different because Transformer used to like him.

"Being a guidance counsellor is not the same as being your teacher."

No kidding. Most teachers won't meet you alone in the janitor's closet. That's about the size of this place.

"I'm part fortune-teller but not a great cheerleader. You might hear me say things like, 'Take chemistry. Take your physics. Take science and math and take biology. Keep all your doors open!' But mostly I'm just an adult who you can speak to, and open your heart to, if you so wish." That sounds romantic, but so far not understanding what the adult Mr. Dawson is talking about seems like the whole point.

"Sorry to disappoint you, I mean, if you came in expecting to hear me spill the conventional crap? That parental stuff. I'm not dealing that in here."

Dealing that. Cool.

"If we progress, through our meetings and over time, I'll help you develop into your own unique someone in this veil of tears…"

Double cool.

"How is your brother these days? I had him here a few years."

"He's okay. We have a band."

"Double fantasy."

"What?"

"Just that you two formed a band. And you're brothers."

"I guess."

"What else is happening in your world?"

"Nothing."

"Think of something."

"I'm a prefect."

"I saw. It's in our file. Not my department. My department is imparting wisdom." He laughs aloud at his own joke. "I just made that up."

I bet.

TRADES

"I'll come watch," Spit says. "But I won't bring my records. You've got nothing I want anyway."

"We've got nothing *we* want," Transformer grumbles as he retrieves the milk crate that contains the dregs of our inheritance. "We should get rid of these roots."

Making trades. The lingo derives from our pre-band existence when Transformer and I would get together with neighbourhood friends and freaks to trade hockey cards. That was the idea: trading and bartering and adding to your collection. The trouble was everybody wanted to trade for Montreal Canadiens players, and nobody would trade one of the Canadiens unless they had doubles. And no one had doubles. Still, it was something to "talk trades" and at least see what everybody "had" and maybe, if you got lucky, to behold a Norris Trophy winner and masticate on their numbers as you read off the biographical details. In the limited time that you held that player card in your hand, you were busy trying not to forget things that would float away in a flash, like whether the player shoots left or right.

"Won't it hurt your uncle's feelings," Spit says, "if you toss his records?"

"He'll never find out." Transformer opens the window and lights a cigarette. "Listens to disco anyway."

Spit stabs a finger down her throat.

"He caught the fever, huh?"

"Delirious."

"That bad?"

"Situation critical."

"Like he's gotta go to hospital?"

Transformer squints as smoke coils before his eyes. "Yeah… it's that bad."

Spit shudders in cold disbelief. "What happened to him?"

"Search me," Transformer says.

While tuning, she sneaks a glance at Bjorn Borg above the headboard. Odd company for Patti Smith? Not really. Bjorno is untouchable. Neil Young—who once anchored my side of the room—had to come down on Transformer's orders. Young is rolled into a tube stored under my bed.

"What crowd are you in with anyway?"

"We're not."

"What do you mean?"

The crowd coming over on Sunday includes this kid Darren we know from Bethune and his friend Nick and the Willey twins who live behind us.

"The trouble is," Transformer says, "nobody wants to hang out with *him*—the pervert. Tell her, Hombre."

"They made me a prefect."

"Who did?" Spit asks.

"My school."

"Oh brother." She hooks an eyebrow. "What is that anyway?"

"A little prick," Transformer provides a handy definition, "who spies for the principal. With authority to make arrests. And give spankings."

"Shut up."

"Is that what you want?"

Spit gives me time to respond.

"No."

"I told him there's a way out of it," Transformer says. "Tell the administration you're in a band and that you're going punk."

"I'm not going punk."

"Yeah, you are."

"You can't *go* punk." Spit comes between us. "This is stupid. Play something. You have a gig coming up. What's your set list?"

Transformer exhales a blue plume over our heads.

"Big rock star," she says.

Another billowing cloud as he runs his hand through his hair. "I'm bagged."

"What are you talking about?"

"The whole thing."

"He means the status quo," I pipe up. "He hates the system."

She rolls her eyes.

"No kidding."

"Yeah. He's had it."

"The only system you need to worry about is the bus system."

He hates that too.

CRIMES

We are at the market. Everybody sits on the floor: the Willey twins Neil and Gavin, Darren, Darren's friend Nick, and Spit. Transformer pokes through Darren's cardboard box first. Darren has a good twenty records that he's ready to trade. But it's mostly the same shit we inherited from Uncle Per. Plus, some Supertramp.

"*Crime of the Century*." Transformer singles out the album. "They got that right."

Nick has brought his green milk crate.

"Why did you bring that, Nick?" Why a whole crate to transport two records?

"In case." Nick has his answer.

"In case what?"

Nick blows his bangs from his eyes. Never mind. The Willey twins don't have much. Neil and Gavin sit cross-legged side by side, trusty wineskins on a string, not saying anything because Spit is in the room. Transformer pokes through their box.

"Where did you get this?" He pulls out Nana Mouskouri. "She looks like our old kindergarten teacher."

Everyone laughs at this except Spit. The idea of kindergarten is preposterous. An *old* kindergarten teacher is ludicrous.

Three beats late, the Willeys confess, "Our mom gave it to us."

"Do you two talk in stereo?"

They do. And they squint when Spit addresses them. They've always been shy around girls. In return, girls treat them anthropologically.

"Leave them alone," Transformer admonishes Spit.

Little does she know Neil and Gavin are pyros. Fire nut-cases. Last summer, the Willeys concocted a pink jelly made with gasoline. Our gang terrorized the neighbourhood at night. Neil and Gavin came up with an idea to set lawns on fire. The Willeys are the closest thing to friends we have. They're harmless, but you don't want to unravel their ire and have identical twins come back during the night to set your house on fire by mistake. Come to think of it, it's not a bad thing that Flowers installed the ladder.

"Does anybody have any LA punk?" Nick inquires.

"I might," says Darren.

Not a chance.

"So is this some kind of nerd club?" Spit says.

"Yeah." The twins get goofy. Loosen.

Transformer takes a second peek inside Darren's box. It used to be good fun, making trades. There was nothing to it.

"Why don't you borrow instead?"

Spit's idea is not a bad one.

"Because making trades is more exciting," I say.

"For you, Hombre, blowing your nose is exciting." For this, Transformer is rewarded with snickers from the half-wits.

"Yeah, for you…" Gavin can't hold it together. "For you a blow job is exciting."

"Yeah, a blow job." His brother Neil sputters into hectic laughter.

"Good luck," Spit says. "I'm leaving." She takes a bow.

"See you," I say.

"The less the merrier," Transformer says.

With Spit's departure, the mood shifts. Darren comes alive and hollers to get the show rolling.

"Come on, somebody make a trade!"

"We will trade this ABBA," Transformer says. "For… what have you got here?" He flips through Darren's box a third time. "April Wine… Bobby Vinton! Did you rob your mom *and* your dad? We'll take…" He turns instead to Nick. "We'll take T Rex."

"No chance," Nick says.

"ABBA comes with a surprise," Transformer says.

"What surprise?"

"We're not telling." Transformer isn't, and I'm not either.

That makes Darren curious. "I'll trade Genesis for Nick's T Rex and then trade you guys the T Rex for ABBA. I'll get it for my mom."

"Sure."

For his mom.

"You want to see the surprise?" Transformer slowly draws the centrefold from the sleeve.

"Miss April," a stereo announcement.

The twins know a thing or two.

Darren says nothing.

The man made a good trade.

CHARITY

Spit telephones before the lesson to ask if it's all right if we do something different today.

"Like what?"

"You'll see, Hombre."

Within fifteen minutes, she's climbing the stairs to our room. She sighs when she puts her box of records down. Sighs a second time upon registering Transformer fastening a safety pin to his sleeve. And upon inhaling the stale air, her pained face says it all: how did she get caught doing charity work for people like us who don't deserve it but need it so badly?

"Boys, get ready… you need to hear all of this."

It's no longer just lessons. Now it's missionary. Because we are undernourished. Underdeveloped. Badly governed. Bankrupt. Spit agrees to loan us more pedals. A pink chorus, a white delay, and a brown box for distortion.

"Until you can play," she says, "you'll need more pedals if you want to sound any good."

Meanwhile, there is our sentimental education: listening to the Buzzcocks, Joy Division, Iggy Pop. The Clash's "London Calling."

"Like it?" Spit asks.

I love the front cover with the punk smashing the stage floor with his guitar like it's bedrock. Who doesn't? Transformer can't sit still. Not with hungry guitars gnashing the air and the kook proclaiming the apocalypse. He makes this tiny run and jumps onto his mattress, raises his foot to kick off the wall, spins and sprints to the other side of the room.

Spit reads the situation. "Classic Hombre," she says as Transformer flies by. "Your big brother here is going to split the atom all by himself and you just sit there, like you're not going to expend an iota of energy."

"I just like to listen," I say.

"Remember, he's a pervert," Transformer says as he whizzes past. "He likes listening to music alone."

True. If possible, I don't even want him around. Especially when I borrow a new record and straightaway take it home and upstairs and put it on the turntable. If Transformer is out, good. I stand away from the speakers, and before any sound comes out, I study the art for clues. What will this sound like? All I need is the music to blow the top off my head. What else changes my world but music? I'm hopeless without music. If the music leaves me cold, then—and this distinguishes me from him because if Transformer doesn't like it, full stop, never again—I apply myself like the pervert I am. I listen again to find something I like: a riff, vocal harmony, the lyrics. Transformer doesn't have the need, but I do. But sometimes it's so bad nothing can save it. Not the guitar riff, not the bass player, not the drums, not the naked mermaids on the front crawling through sludge. *What a fucking rip-off! There is nothing going on! This music sucks!* Sometimes it's as if the group went into the studio just to get depressed. I find myself gawking at the four members photographed, wondering who is who. *Fuckin' hell. No liner notes either! The bunch of losers.* I can't forgive that. Sacred duty says I spread the word. *They suck! Bollocks! They aren't for real!*

Spit puts on the next record. "Hear that?" She's pointing to the speaker as this band we already know goes walking on the moon.

"That's a digital delay, plus a Flange." She's a talking technician. We're still enjoying ourselves when she changes it up again. The Ramones. Black Flag. The Buzzcocks again and, finally—Spit's very excited about this—Siouxsie and the Banshees.

"Do you know what a banshee is?"

"Not really." Not at all. Really.

"She's a witch. A spirit in Irish folklore."

"How do you know?"

"I just do," she says. "You guys have a big family. I don't."

It doesn't make sense. But ours is the age.

"Put the Ramones back on."

Spit ignores Transformer's request. She implores him to give Siouxsie more time, making it sound for a second like Siouxsie is her best friend.

"Have either of you heard of the expression 'to scream like a banshee'?"

Nope.

"It's when the banshees sit outside the house at night and make this high-pitched crying sound."

"What do they do that for?"

"To scare the shit out of you probably." That's Transformer.

I'm thinking. "They sound like our Tomten," I say.

"Your what?"

"Tomten. These ex-cons we have from Swedish folklore. Little guys on parole from Santa's workshop," Transformer says.

Around Christmas, Flowers plasters the kitchen walls with Astrid Lindgren posters. We get lots of winter scenes featuring the wizened old men known as Tomten prowling golden straw barnyards. Them with the ruddy faces and solid white beards protect the farm from intruders. Tomten use a kind of good cheer to ward off predators. For sure, Tomten are frightening sprites.

"Yeah, maybe," Spit says. "Banshees can smell death." Gives me a hard stare. "They wait outside your house and scream like murder."

"I get it," Transformer says.

"Anyway," Spit says. "Time to jam."

We've had our dose of Siouxsie. I'm the first to pick up a guitar.

"Ramones!" Transformer heckles me before I get going.

But I fingerpick "Norwegian Wood" instead.

"That's not how you play it," Spit says, outstretching a panicked hand to mute my strings.

"Ding-dong, London calling," Transformer enunciates, all English-y.

"Classic Hombre," Spit says it again.

"Phony Beatlemania!"

Sure, but up until last December, when he was still at Bethune, Transformer took after Mr. Dawson and was a dedicated follower of Lennonism. Even if Mr. Dawson is into heavier stuff like Zeppelin and Cream and a bit of Sabbath, the Beatles and Lennon especially are a beloved of our high school guidance counsellor. For Dawson, the first invasion changed life on earth. Things changed, but still that all feels like yesterday.

Transformer steps on the distortion pedal and begins whacking at bar chords to incinerate my rendition of the classic. In retaliation, I flick on the chorus with my foot, and we're off, no handbrake, racing down the fretboard, on a road of mutual destruction.

Spit won't join in. She's displeased. In a bit, we stop in our tracks.

"When are you going to start taking this more seriously?"

We trade blank expressions.

"You need practice. To really work on your playing."

I look down at my fingers. Aren't they raw enough?

"Because when I get my band together," Spit says, "I want to be able to rely on you as back-up."

"Us?"

"You want your own band?"

She ignores both our questions. "First, though, you'll need mop-tops."

And what's that? My expression is asking.

"Silly, it's when you get your hair cut like George or Paul or Ringo into a cute crown so that when we perform the local moms hold themselves screaming like they're melting. I expect real mayhem at our concerts."

"I'll scream at your concerts if you want," Transformer says, unwanted.

"What's wrong with our hair?" I say.

Hers is spiked. "I bet you do each other's?"

"No, we don't."

"Who does it then… your mother?" She's got us there. "Forget it. I don't care. Keep molesting it. But when I have my band, one thing is for sure: my back-up boys will wear crowns."

"So you really do want a band?"

For the record, this is our second longest conversation with Spit, and the longest conversation we have had with any visitor to our room.

"What do you think? That you and Transformer are unique?"

For the record, that's not true. That's not what I was thinking. I recover to ask another question. "What will you call yourself?"

"Spit."

"Original."

She snorts. "Well, yaw."

"Why 'Spit'?"

"Because it's what people get rid of—and it's disgusting."

Transformer stares at me with his molested hair.

"So why are *you* Spit?" Transformer glares again for some reason.

"You really want to know?" She rolls up her sleeve. "Want me to show you?"

Her forearm is marked like a fretboard. "Happy?"

This bird has flown.

I strum a tune.

She still hasn't answered the question though, not really.

Slouched against the wall, Transformer shoots his legs forward off the bed. "Why did you have to ask her about all that? Leave her alone next time. But anyway, no harm done."

"What do you mean?"

"I don't know."

Neither do I.

"She'll be fine."

I guess.

"I'm serious." He rips off his shirt and grabs his left nipple. "Look at these."

"What?"

"Really look."

I look harder.

"Do you have any hairs?"

Not yet.

Transformer puts his shirt back on. "Your turn is coming, Hombre. You're right behind me. Smoke?"

Outside on the roof, Transformer sparks a match and begins rubbing his ciggy against his shirt, turning it to sharpen the end. He's playing with fire. Making a show. Showing off for me.

"How do you feel now?" I speak.

"What you mean?"

"Nothing."

"Then why did you ask?"

The things you don't know about people aren't supposed to hurt you, but you always end up finding out. He scares me sometimes.

PSYCHO

Candy insists Transformer is becoming a fascist, especially now that he plays electric guitar, and that I'm the nice one.

"But I'm not."

"But you are, Hombre."

Shoot me, I'm already a prefect.

"How is school going?"

"I don't know. OK, I guess."

The reputation of a nice prefect will get me killed.

"Have you met anybody new this year?"

"Not that I know of."

She smiles a bit.

"Anyway. Don't let him control you."

"He doesn't."

Rather than someone nice, I'd like to become known as a psycho. Not a psycho killer, just a psycho. Or at least for being lonely a lot of the time, if that's something you can get known for.

"That's good. I'm happy to hear that."

She hasn't heard anything I wanted to say.

PUSHER

Here she comes again.

Flowers breaks in, empties the laundry basket on the floor, and exits. She knows the drill. We don't stop for visitors. We're getting ready for the gig. Busy today jamming Transformer's new song called "Johnny Worm."

"It's about a pusher," Transformer informs me.

"Isn't he supposed to be a pusher man?"

"Not always. You can say pusher."

I have my doubts.

"Let's do another," he says. "Do you have anything?"

I have a few spare parts lying around, but try fitting pieces together without a spark. It doesn't work that way.

"Let's just keep digging," Transformer says, but honestly is digging enough? I say we need equipment like a microphone. Using the standing lamp and singing into a light bulb is getting tiresome, though Transformer doesn't seem to mind it. Last time I complained, he made me lead singer. He called it a promotion.

A good two hours into this afternoon's digging, I start mumbling tired gibberish to orphan chords, and right away Transformer mutes his guitar.

"Wait. What's that?" Him with the keen ears.

"Nothing."

"You were singing *something*."

"I said it was nothing."

"Don't whine. Start over."

But Flowers reappears at the door, a spectator, not demanding our attention, which is mostly her style, to remain part of the scenery. She never complains about the noise. She's a serious fan. If anything, she cares too much. She hovers around, levitates to unconditional love. In the old days, if Flowers came knocking at the door to our room, still breathless from hurrying up the stairs, we knew it was to announce, "The tennis is on." This meant our private Viking was live on television. Björn Borg was playing a tennis match against Jimmy Connors on red clay at the French Open, or Borg was jousting with John McEnroe on the green hardcourts at the US Open, or the shy topspin king was skipping over the grass to receive the big shiny Wimbledon trophy once more. When the tennis was on, we hurried down the stairs to join the Swedes and Candy before the television set, primed to catch sight of our boy in his white shorts, with his long hair pressed into a headband and Donnay racket resting across the top of the net. During match play, Morfar colour-commented. He often repeated that Borg was from a broken home. That young Borg practised by hitting balls against his garage door. Morfar incited us to do the same—to hit balls in the driveway. He even came out and stopped the tennis balls from running down into the street. Hour after hour of practice and real commitment was all we needed to stay out of trouble and become champion players like Borg. We had it in our blood. We were half Swedish. Still, it surprised everybody that one year Transformer and I were seeded fourth at the Dorval Open. We played in the under-twelve boys' doubles category. I served underhand and we lost our first match. Transformer took a bird.

"Remember that, boys?" Flowers says, forever fond of yesteryear.

"Ancient history," Transformer says.

When we watched tennis, the Swedes served coffee as we cut mille-feuilles in plates on our lap with a fork and knife. Mormor sat in the corner whence she would hiss each time Borg hit the ball.

"Nay, nay, he won't do it, he won't win, nay, nay, nay—"

Morfar would shush her.

"Nay, nay, he won't…"

"Shusshht!"

There was a back and forth between them across an invisible net.

"Nay, nay, he won't do it this time."

"Shusshht!"

"Nay. He won't win."

Nay, nay. In the end, it was mostly always nay. And Mormor was counting on Borg not winning. On him losing. It was safer that way. Hoping for a win would be asking for too much. It would be asking for trouble. So that when Borg would win, the room would fill with palpable dread. Bad luck was upon us. We'd need protection from evil spirits from the Tomten.

Flowers loiters at the door, staring too long at the Expos pennant above my headboard. I'm about to ask what's wrong when Transformer takes the initiative.

"Just spit it out," he says.

She comes to, returns from a side trip down memory lane. "I was just thinking. You can move the band down to the living room when you add a drummer. I don't mind."

Who said anything about a drummer?

"Well, it sounds very good, boys."

"It sounds very good, Hombre," Transformer grumbles after she exits.

Praise is the kiss of death.

ALIENS

Talking at night in bed when my voice doesn't sound like my own voice. With the lights off before sleep, I'll say anything. "Can I ask you something?"

"Shoot."

"Do you get lonely?"

"What?"

"Forget it."

"What are you talking about?"

"Nothing." I'll be awake now for a while on my side of the moon. "Do you think we'll ever need a drummer?"

"We might someday," Transformer answers, matter-of-factly.

One day, someday. Someday will change us. Things won't be the same. Someday.

"We could ask one of the Willeys to be on drums," I say.

"Which one?"

"I don't know."

It's a problem. Mrs. Willey used to dress them in different colours, Neil in brown and red and Gavin in green and blue. Older and free to choose their own clothes, the twins now wear the same thing. Same colour pants and shirts. I've known them longest, and even I have trouble telling them apart.

"There must be somebody else we could…"

"Only Spit." I get up and thumb through our collection.

"Hey," Transformer says to my back. "What do you really think of Spit?"

Ignoring him, I slide out *Rubber Soul.*

"Eh?"

"I like her."

"Liking is for babies."

Then I'm a baby. I'm a baby who misses the records we liked before the inheritance from Uncle Per and before we got to know Spit—times *when we were little*, as Flowers likes to say. Times when I couldn't shape a chord, times when instead of forming the band we played tennis and took drowning lessons at the DRA. In such ancient times as these, Transformer still put on Joni Mitchell, and I'd get drenched just from listening to her voice. Flowers, vacuuming the living room downstairs, would catch wind of "Both Sides Now" and hurry upstairs so that we could listen to that song together. When the song was over, she would squeeze my hand. I'd shiver. It was senseless.

I scoot back to my side of the room with *Rubber Soul* in my hands. "Two weeks before the gig."

"Nervous?"

"I guess." More than a bit, actually.

"Piece of cake."

What does Transformer know about it? He's taken to gigging like old hat. Like he's been there and done that. Like he's a vet.

Lying in bed, I study the record's front cover, and the only Beatle looking me in the eye is John. Which is enough to convince me that John Lennon came up with the idea of *Rubber Soul* and that he, dead John Lennon, wants me to think hard about that.

What does it mean to have a rubber soul?

Eh nice guy, what does it mean?

DREAMERS

The sun kicked in the window.

Morning has broken.

I had a dream last night that kept taking me under and rolling me over. It was exhausting, like swimming against an undertow. I couldn't escape. The whole time, there was this blurry figure watching me struggle. I kept going back under, hoping he would go away. Each time I opened my eyes, he was standing there and seemed interested in me.

"What did he look like?"

Like you, Transformer. The peeping Transformer. But should I say?

"It was hard to see."

But I'm sure it was him. Standing over me. Or was it a dream?

"Did this figure say anything?"

He did.

"I don't remember."

"Well, did he do anything?"

"He just stood there… I guess."

For a long time.

"Then what's the big deal?"

"It was creepy."

"What does that prove?"

"Nothing."

"Get over it."

I'm trying. Sunshine on a Sunday morning helps. Transformer is up early and flipping through a magazine. Flowers is blasting George Frideric Handel. "Zadok the Priest"!

I go, "What kind of dreams do you have?"

"Normal ones. Of setting the house on fire, and of murdering dad."

"Funny."

"I'm not joking."

Those pages flipping make the sound of faint cuts.

"Have you told Flowers?"

"It's none of her business."

Murdering dad might be. That's not possible. Still.

"What are you reading?" I ask.

"*Hit Parader*."

Of course.

"Who's in it?"

"It doesn't matter."

It's an effort to be alive in the morning. He won't say.

Not the green, white, and orange flag. Not the block-lettered instructions. SQUEEZE MY LEMONS. Below the belt. Not the mirror behind the door that warps my face into a butterfly. Not the fact she has a Fender twin amplifier. Not the bass guitar stored beside her Gretsch. Not the red drum set crowded into the corner.

"What are you looking at?"

But him. Led Zep's frontman on stage at Madison Square Garden. Him, half lion, holding the microphone like Dionysus flaunting a glass. Him, half beasty. Spit is all talk about new wave and punk and obscure bands I haven't heard of, but the dead ringer is poster boy above her headboard. That's what jump-starts a mental step backwards upon entering her room for the first time.

"Nothing," I say. "Where did you get all this stuff?"

"From my brother. After he moved out. He can get anything at the store. Someday I want to work there. They have a studio in the back."

"A recording studio?"

"Aw, yeah. Eight tracks."

I unclip my case. Taking a private lesson was her idea. Something she urged me to do before the gig. For one thing, she wants to hear the Ibanez through her amp.

"It has tubes," Split declares, patting the top of the Fender and next showing off the tiny light bulbs tucked inside the back on a small ledge. The thing comes alive when she flicks the switch. It stirs and hums with power, a heavy creature on rollers sharing the space with us. Spit kicks a guitar pedal across the floor.

"Try that out."

I plug in and we start jamming, her sitting on the bed and me on a chair. The whole time, I'm messing with the purple pedal at my feet.

"The Police use it," she says.

Duh, I know that already. I'm just getting going—trying things out—when suddenly she stops.

"What do you want to do?"

"I don't know."

"Does Transformer know you're here?"

"I guess…" My guitar weighs a heavy ton in my lap. "I don't know. He's out, doing the route."

"Isn't my house on your route?"

The birds—no. I stare at the drum set. Wish she would stop talking. She plays drums. He'll want to know.

"Why not?" She's teasing, giving me a faux loving look.

"Just because it isn't."

"Oh boy, you know what you are?" Chews her lip. "Forget it." Instead of following her initial line of inquiry, she pulls a little paper bag out of nowhere and pinches a brown piece of something.

"Want to do shrooms?"

I pretend like I didn't catch that, but it's obvious I did.

She waits me out, proffering her open palm.

"Not right now."

"Right. Another time." She inches back on her bum against the wall and shoves the bag down behind the bed.

We should play guitar, shouldn't we? That's why I came over, for a lesson. To remind her, I strike a few chords. But the inquisition continues.

"Are you two virgins?"

"No."

"That's not what Candy said."

"Candy listens to Top 40."

"She's your big sister."

Instead of maintaining eye contact—torture—I stare at him above the headboard: Robert the Lionheart. Below Plant's beltline in the "dial 69 to get out" area, the material is worn through, blue jean faded to white.

"I've got a great idea!"

Lemons, my ass.

"We should go together! *The Song Remains the Same*! At Cinema V. Then we can do shrooms."

Coconuts.

"I mean it. That would be perfect."

"Maybe."

"Promise?"

I've never been to a cinema downtown. Never trekked to Cinema V in NDG. That's two buses and a metro ride from here. We'd have to transfer twice.

The tubes are letting off heat, and now she begins pulling her sweatshirt off but keeps talking with it still covering half her head.

"Do you remember what I was telling you and Transformer… about the kind of band I want? I've been thinking it through. I'll put you on bass and Transformer on drums."

"I don't play bass."

"Don't worry. One note at a time. That's how you play bass. It's easy. Anyway, I was going to say we're only doing instrumentals."

"What do you mean?"

"Just me on guitar, you on bass, and Transformer on the drums."

"Transformer doesn't play drums."

"What's wrong with you?"

"Nothing."

"It's just an idea."

"I know."

"I was just *talking*…!"

"What?"

"Fuck, are you on drugs?"

"No."

"Well, I offered."

"Sorry."

"Don't say you're sorry."

I shut up.

She says, "Lots of songs begin with the music until the lead vocalist comes in, right? That's how you write songs, right?"

For me, sometimes the process is like having a chorus of banshees screaming in my ear. It's a bit nerve-wracking.

"…first you come up with a riff. Add vocals, then bass. But what if the singer can't sing it? What if the lyrics are wrong? You throw out your song, and everything you worked on is lost. Just because the singer can't sing, the band ditches the entire song, but in my group that won't happen."

It doesn't make sense. Once again, I am speechless.

"Wake up!"

"Sorry."

"What's wrong with you?"

"Nothing."

"Jesus."

"Well, don't take a bird." There I said it. Take a bird. Pull a bird. The expression has nothing to do with the bird streets where Spit lives. She stretches out her legs. A long passage of silence swallows us from head to toe, and when we come out of it, we've landed someplace else.

"I have a lot of problems with my appearance," Spit says. "I'm short, so I look fat." She nods towards the door. "That mirror makes me look tall." Now reaches under the bed. "Look at these." Hands me a bunch. Magazine cut-outs. Photographs of glamour brides. Models in bikinis. "I have more." She retrieves her second box. "I've been collecting for years. I have lots of energy."

I don't follow.

"Probably too much energy."

She begins knocking her knees and banging her legs on the floor like she's in spasm and can't control it. "I'm going to Antarctica."

"You are?"

"Someday."

"Why?"

"Because nobody lives there. I'd be alone."

She talks like everything makes sense, but it doesn't. It's time to leave, get home in time for dinner, but she has a different idea. "Let's tell jokes."

I hate telling jokes. Too much pressure.

"What's pink and red and sits in the corner on the kitchen counter?"

"I don't know."

"Baby in a blender."

Makes sense.

"I have another."

Figures.

"How do you know when your baby is dead? The dog plays with it more. I have another one," she adds breathlessly. "What bounces up and down at 100 mph?"

Dead-baby jokes. That's what she's got. Transformer used to tell them about a year ago, when they first caught on and lots of people started repeating them around school. Dead babies were all the rage.

"You don't have to tell sick jokes," I say, and I mean it partly in her own defence, if that makes sense.

"You're right. I don't have to tell jokes or have babies." She nails this statement with a vengeance as if being childless at fifteen could be her claim to fame. "I don't want to get married… and be forced to have children and go directly to jail. Without passing Go. You do not collect any money. You go directly out to the fat farm."

No wonder she wants to leave for Antarctica.

"I should go." I begin to pack my guitar away.

"Don't be a baby," she says.

There are a lot of things about Spit that I don't understand. Instrumentals. Cuts. Her jokes, as though babies make her mad at the world. And she pretends she's in a band but she's not. Not really.

AUDITION

Fresh blood is called for after all. A human sacrifice to appease the gods before the gig.

"Should we advertise?"

"Where?"

He knows where. The only place we can afford.

"Nah, nobody reads it. What did Spit say?"

"About?"

"Finding us a drummer."

"I didn't ask."

Squints in sour disbelief. "Why not?"

"I forgot."

"Are you on drugs?"

Everybody asks. I should have taken the shrooms when Spit offered. I'm sure I could play drums while on shrooms.

"Don't we know anybody else?" Transformer says, sounding really disgusted with our poverty of friends, the inexistence of a private Rolodex.

"Just Darren." Transformer knows him from Bethune and from—

"The Darren kid we did trades with? Chubby with acne and a twelve-string?"

"Yeah, that's him." Acne abounds but Darren is permanently under siege. There's not one section of his face that is clear. He gets pimples in his ears.

"Darren's played guitar since he was in grade seven."

"That means he's Muddy Waters?"

"No."

"What's he into? Echo and the Bunnymen? Joy Division? Costello? The Fall—they're not bad. The Stranglers? Hombre, I'm not convinced… Might we have a Genesis fan?"

Does he not remember the day of the trades? What Darren had and had not in his box. Last year, I went for a sleepover at Darren's and curled up for the night in the little space behind the dry bar in the basement. Darren put on that Supertramp album with the grand piano caked with snow in the high mountains.

"He's into lots of stuff," I bluff, doing my best while under observation to sound vague as I try to remember the full range of Darren's collection. Genesis there was. Styx? Wasn't there a lot of Yes?

"Nobody is pure," I say, proud to land on an idea of my own.

"What is that supposed to mean?" Transformer says.

"Everybody comes from somewhere."

"You sound like an old man."

Transformer is the one who looks like Morfar.

"All right. Darren can jam. But that doesn't mean he's in the band."

And who is going to tell Darren that? Nobody. Nobody is going to explain to Darren the logic and morality of our little understanding. Least of all Transformer.

"He doesn't get in just because the boy has a twelve-string."

"I get it. New blood was your idea."

"No, it wasn't."

He gets the last word. But yes, it was.

BLOOD

"So what are we called?" Darren asks right after flipping the latches of his guitar case and lifting out his twelve-string.

Transformer turns away, hard-stares the wall. Instead of acknowledging the question, I ask Darren, "How do you tune that thing?"

"Oh, it's easy," Darren says. "String by string like a normal guitar."

"What does it sound like?"

"Like this." And he begins plucking harmonics on the twelfth fret. His guitar sounds bright.

"So what do you want to do?" Darren is game for anything. Transformer plays Darren "Fuck Creation," and next I show him my new one called "If the Sun." For the next thirty minutes, we review our back catalogue and then, before we can stop him, Darren brings up something of his own and tries to feed it to us. We're not that hungry. Silence looms. Discouraged, Darren begins picking the corny intro to a Yes song.

"Harmonics," Transformer says.

"I can show you," Darren says.

"Another life," Transformer says. "I gotta go."

It's almost four. Time to deliver.

"See you," Darren says.

"Yeah."

With Transformer gone, Darren says, "This is so cool."

"What is?"

"Being in a band!"

But he's not in the band. He's just in our room. There's a difference.

"When's our next practice?"

Somebody ought to explain it to him.

The autopsy begins that night, with Transformer etherized upon his bed like a dirty tired punk.

"He's not in the band."

"I know."

"Then tell him. He's your friend."

Not really. He's not even in my grade. Closer to Transformer in age.

"His talent could be useful."

"Useful for what?"

Useful for tuning our guitars, for one thing. I'd like to offer Darren moral support, but I'm not sure how. I get really quiet.

After a bit, Transformer says, "You're in a bad mood."

"No, I'm not."

Transformer gets up. He selects a record, then returns to his bed.

"I want you to listen to her voice."

"I'm listening."

I'm forced like this all the time. Night classes of compulsory listening.

"I'll make you a bet," Transformer says. This is his new thing: making bets. "One day, I'll sing a duet with Patti."

Interesting bet for someone who talks a lot about taking a vow of silence.

"You don't even like singing."

"With Patti, there would be no problem."

Patti. With Patti, of course not. He's smitten by the spooky waif. I'd like to take that poster down. Sometimes it's hard going to sleep under Patti's hard stare, with the doves settled upon her twiggy fingers. She's supposed to be waving?

"Why do you like her so much?"

"Are you stupid?" Transformer sits up, then lays back down: "Just listen." He holds the album cover aloft, straight-arms it overhead. "Listen to her, Hombre."

"I am."

"Really listen."

"I said I am. You be quiet."

It's he who doesn't listen. It's he who won't lay off. I stare up at the ceiling, and Transformer slips away. Suddenly, all is quiet on the Transformer front. And now it begins, this long period, this interlude before sleeping, in our tomb of make-believe. We tire ourselves out by making cheeky bet after cheeky bet. Satisfied that future life is nothing more than a game of chance with an infinite number of squares on the board. Transformer is faking sleep on his square. A royal Tutankhamun. I'm dead quiet over here in my square Neil Young world. The real Patti Smith roosts on our wall. Everyone occupies a square. The future is divided with empty squares between us. When it's time to move forward, we blow on our fingers. Roll the dice. And jump ahead. Sing a duet. Play.

"You'll probably do it," I say, meaning he's brave enough, thinking he's crazy enough to believe in himself.

Transformer laughs and at the same time growls, meaning he's pleased with the situation, which in turn makes me feel happy for him.

The record stops playing. For a while longer, we sink deeper into sands of silence. Finally, Transformer comes to: "Being quiet comes from inside. You understand that, right?

Not really.

"Like being punk. Punk comes from inside too. Punk is not about the haircuts and paperclips stuck in your nose. Punk might be about training doves or something."

"I know."

But is that possible?

"You're the quiet one, Hombre."

The nice quiet one.

"Your new stuff is really good."

"Thanks."

"You don't have to say thanks."

"I know."

"I bet you had all these songs inside you from the beginning."

"From the beginning of what?"

"Probably from the beginning of you."

That's fucking weird. In this freak mellowing of Transformer's mind, I see my opportunity to ask a delicate question. "What do you think is wrong with Spit?"

"What do you mean?"

"She says a lot of things."

"So?"

"You saw what she did to herself."

"Lots of people do that."

Do they?

"It's her right."

I begin rubbing my skin.

"Maybe," I begin, because I want to know more, "she thinks it's going to make her feel better?"

"Grow up," Transformer says.

Lights out.

POET

Flowers is down in the yard weeding the garden. We're on the roof. I went to sleep thinking about Spit and woke up with this song in my head. It makes no sense. Transformer sits along the ledge, legs dangling, rolling a glass bottle over his six strings, playing homemade slide guitar, while I sing.

Down it comes
Down it pours
Sleepy sheets of rain

My back aches
I'm pitchforked
I slant into the house

"That's good, Hombre. You're becoming a poet."

More and more often, what I do is good by him. I do feel something changing, something growing inside.

"He's going to be the next Leonard Cohen," Flowers says from below in the garden.

"No, he's not." Transformer rolls the bottle, the low strings clang.

"Well, I think so." Flowers stands, stretches her back.

"Your opinion…" Transformer says, then in a whisper to me: "Doesn't matter."

"Especially," Flowers says, "if you boys stick with acoustic guitar."

There's always something new
Changing my point of view
There's always… something… new
I saw that long before I met you

"You sound old-fashioned," Transformer says, "but I like it." He whistles. "It's a natural."

"It's a very good one," Flowers confirms just as Candy appears in the yard from around the side gate.

Flowers announces to the new arrival, "Hombre has a new song."

"Where did he get it?" Candy asks.

"He got it at Steinberg's in the vegetable section." Transformer lights a cigarette. "Better hurry and copyright it."

"Copyright kills," I say so semi-automatically. Covers are for cocks and copyright kills. These hard truths are self-evident. We have a running joke. At first, the idea of copyright was hilarious. It's a little insane that we can own the right to copy our own shit.

"It's for corpses." Transformer tosses his cigarette.

"Hey!" Flowers yells from below. "You're going to start a fire."

"I'm trying," Transformer says.

"Asshole," Candy says.

"Don't talk like that." Flowers is standing hands on her hip and stretching sideways.

"Sorry," I say.

"It's him," Candy says. "Not you."

"It's me, the number of the beast," says the number of the beast.

Flowers shakes it off. The garden is her retreat. Her realm of perennials runs down the side of the house.

"Hey," Candy shouts. "Is Darren playing the gig?"

"Do pigs fly?"

"Why not?"

"Because."

"That's a big loss." Candy blocks sun with her hand and proposes a theory to me. "He makes you sound better."

Different, maybe.

"I'm going in." Transformer mumbles, and as I follow him offstage, he conspires to whisper: "You better tell Darren that he *never was* in the band. Set him straight…"

"Why me?"

"You're the poet."

I don't want to be.

"The words will come to you."

I doubt that.

DADS

Next private lesson, the dead-baby jokes fall off the menu.

"But I thought Darren was your friend?"

"He is."

Spit snorts. "I feel sorry for him." She stares at me like she can finally see I'm an earthworm. Just a worm, not even Johnny Worm the pusher man.

"I feel sorry for him too."

"Then do something."

"I can't."

"Has anybody ever let you down?"

"I guess my dad died."

"You *guess*?"

"When I was just a kid."

"You're still a kid."

"Actually, just after I was born."

"That's not what I meant. He didn't do it on purpose, did he?"

"No."

From across the river of time, it's happening again: Flowers pushing the carriage, my dad holding Candy's hand when he collapses inside the big dome.

"My dad left us, but we're better off without him." Spit

pulls out a bag of jellybeans. "He wasn't good to my mom or me."

What kind of dad is that?

"He's still alive though, right?"

"Yeah, but he doesn't count. He just doesn't."

Spit grazes the skin of my hand with her own. "I don't want to talk about it."

Neither do I.

DEBT

Darren catches up with me at the bus stop down from Bethune, along the service road in Dollard.

"Are we still practising?"

"We've been jamming. Transformer and I worked on a few songs."

"I would have come…" Darren is hurting. My words aren't coming. I'm no poet. "If I'm not in the band anymore, say it. Tell me to my face. Just say it."

When I say it, Darren's acne turns a deeper shade of red. That wasn't easy. But on the bus ride home, after he gets off, I begin to feel impressed with myself. Don't the best bands depend on having a ruthless streak? I might have cruelty in me after all. I climb the stairs in a rush to find Transformer and tell him about Darren. He's sitting cross-legged on the desk, wearing the headphones. Hands clasping both sides of his head. Face askew, moaning.

"Transformer! What are you listening to?"

He lifts the headphones off and the Electric Light Orchestra bleeds into the atmosphere.

"We have to pay our debt," Transformer says.

"You mean dues."

Transformer dabs his eyes with his shirtsleeve.

"Are you crying?"

"No."

He is.

"I just told him. I told Darren."

A face inscribed with melancholy. Melancholy verging into sickness. Transformer shifts off the desk and lowers himself onto the bed. That's the sign for me to go ahead. My turn is next.

"I told Darren."

"I heard you the first time."

Transformer scoots back over to lower the headphones around my ears, then taps me on the top of my head.

"Farewell," he says.

I close my eyes and attend to this concoction by Jeff "sugar-sweet" Lynn. The studio Einstein with a trim beard and buzzy hair, with the soft hands for blending violins with disco bass and guitars and sickly harmonies.

We all pay our debt to society for the things we do.

POOF

"I want to tell you about your father" is how she always begins. "Your father had a heart condition. He found that out very early. In that sense, he was lucky. He was worried about having children."

She pauses, stares at us both, bewildered, as if here we are now suddenly: two of the children our father was frightened of having. At the same time, poof, he is gone.

"He wanted to take care of you."

"Mom. We know."

"I know you know. But listen. He was terrified that he would not get to see you grow up. But when Catherine was born, it made us so happy. And now he's going to miss your first show."

"Don't make Hombre cry," Transformer says. "He's a poet."

"It's important to remember the past," she says, "especially now that you are older and making things. Not everything lasts forever. Did you know that the day he had his heart attack, there were over half a million visitors to Notre Dame Island?"

I can't think clearly. She makes it sound crazy, as though those half a million were on hand to witness his fatal attack—more people than who attended Woodstock, maybe.

"Go to sleep early tonight, boys." She slips her voice through the door. "Tomorrow is a big day."

"Relax," he says. "It's not Carnegie Hall."

But she's already gone.

SULTANS

Uncle Per drives us to the gig. We sit in the back of his car, guitars crowded upfront on the passenger side. Ready or not, here we come.

"So, boys, how do you feel?"

Transformer makes a face. "How *do we feel*, Hombre?"

I couldn't eat lunch. My legs are trembling.

"You'll be all right," Uncle Per says, "when the lights go up."

"Yeah." Transformer does it again. "When the lights blow up, things will be fire."

Uncle Per flicks on the car radio. Rolls the dial. Transformer stares out the side window.

"Wonder if Megan will come? This is her beat."

"Her what?"

Transformer ignores me. Uncle Per turns up the volume. "This is some good music." He puts eyes on me in the rear-view mirror. "Eh, Hombre? Isn't this good?"

"Well, it ain't no disco," Transformer says.

Uncle Per gives me a second chance to respond. "What do you think, Hombre? Will it be a hit?"

Uncle Per must be out of it. "This is really old," I say— the song *is already* a hit. FM radio was all over it last year.

The band is ratchet tight. The guitarist plays ultra clean. I'm inclined to believe he tidies up his room straight after riffing in it or something.

Transformer whistles. "He's a bona fide technician, that's for sure."

"What's a technician?" Uncle Per asks.

"He's a musician," I enlighten Uncle Per. "A technician is a musician."

"Then, if I may ask, what are you two?"

"Idiots."

"He means idiot savants."

"Oh, really?" Uncle Per sounds hopeful. Right then, the DJ intones, "That was Dire Straits from 1979 with…"

"Lame name," Transformer says.

"Technically," Uncle Per says.

"Sultans?" I stammer. "What is a Sultan?" But nobody is listening, and I don't expect an answer. The Veterans' Hospital looms ahead. A brown brick building, about twelve storeys high. The reality that we're playing *in there* makes me nauseous. That it's happening today. For real. Makes me breathless. Uncle Per brings the car around to the front entrance, where thankfully there is no overhanging marquee. No bright lights announcing: *Today! Because. One matinee only!*

Parked by the curb, I notice an ambulance. Talk about an omen. I spot Spit hanging around, off to the side. Good on her for taking the bus.

"One of your groupies?" Uncle Per says.

It was only a matter of time before that joke got killed.

"Thanks for the lift," I say, and the band climbs out.

"Hurry," Spit says. "Upstairs."

"Have a good performance." Uncle Per leans forward over the steering wheel and waves.

"Your uncle is funny," Spit says as we enter the elevator together.

Soon we are on our way up to the fifth-floor sunroom, me hugging my acoustic, Transformer lugging his guitar and amp, Spit pressing multiple buttons.

"We ought to have groupies," Transformer says. "Uncle Per is right."

"What?" Spit says.

The doors slide open on the second floor. "Groupies," he repeats.

"To sell T-shirts!" Spit gets it.

"Propaganda," says Transformer.

"We don't even have T-shirts," I say.

"The emperor's clothes," says Transformer.

The doors blink at the fourth floor.

"One day." Spit's fidgeting. "Are you ready?"

"Hombre, are we ready?"

"I wish I had my electric guitar for this."

"Don't be a baby."

The doors slide apart. The amp has two inputs, but we blew a channel last week in rehearsal. I'm back to digging with my acoustic. We exit the elevator and begin walking in the direction of the sunroom. At the end of the hall, the site ahead is hollowed out in a haze of cigarette smoke. Waiting there for us are about fifteen people sitting at the tables. In-patients. Residents. Veterans. Casualties of war. The enemy as far as I'm concerned. No sight of Candy. We drop our things by the old piano.

"You better get going," Spit says, "and set up."

Transformer gets busy making his amplifier come alive. No hesitation with him. The staff is wheeling in more zombies even as we are getting set to blast them away.

"I guess everyone's a doctor here or something," I say, looking around.

"Or *something*." Spit is a quick wit.

"Candy isn't." Transformer knows his facts. "She's mental, not medical."

I look around some more. It's my first time in a hospital. It's like an apartment building with small bedrooms, or like a school where the students are older than the teachers and have nothing to do.

"Just because the staff wear white doesn't mean everybody's a doctor or nurse," Spit says, without somehow beginning her sentence with *for your information*.

"Björn Borg and John McEnroe wear a lot of white," Transformer says.

That gets me laughing, but not Transformer: he doesn't know a joke even when he tells one; most people eventually notice that about him.

"Sorry, I'm late." Sister Candy appears, carrying a tray and little paper cups. "I brought you some juice."

"Thanks, Candy."

"Is there any place to change?" Transformer asks.

"You mean like a dressing room?"

"Yeah."

"No. Do you have a costume?"

He's already turned his back to slip on his headband.

"You're not going to wear that, are you?" Spit says.

He is. She turns to me. "You look great, Hombre."

I feel less than zero. Candy puts the tray down on the piano top. "This is for the band. Spit, you too." Dispossessed of her burden, Candy slides both hands into her back pockets. She'll be sticking around backstage while the band gets ready.

"So are you going to introduce us?" I ask Candy.

"Before you go on? Sorry, I can't." She points to the Colonel, as she calls him. "I have to take care of that guy." The Colonel flips a bandaged paw. "You'll be okay," Candy reassures me. "You guys can begin whenever you like."

This doesn't sound right to me—that we can start playing whenever we want, almost as if nobody cares or will notice. Yet Candy sneaks off to her Colonel. She snaps a lighter and holds it to his cigarette, which is stuck to the end of a length of tubing. The smoke draws into his lungs as the Colonel inhales through a hole in his throat. Candy already described this set-up more than once, but it's crazy and sad to watch in real life. Meanwhile, Spit is kneeling on all fours, using a roll of masking tape to mark two little "X"s on the floor: the spot where Transformer should stand, the position where I should sing from. This bit of mise-en-scène accomplished, she takes her juice and walks to the back of the room. She'll do sound from back there.

"There'll be no pogoing or moshing," says Transformer, untangling a patch cord. "But you have to hand it to them, Hombre… Some of these vets have done trench warfare. Isn't that the same thing? Punks and the poets of the Great War have nothing on this crew."

What is he talking about? Punks and poets? Pogoing and moshing? Transformer speaks his mind as he fiddles with his pedals and patch chords, an arrangement laid out on the floor as an extension of his distracted self. As for myself, I have nothing so complicated to untangle or set up. In no man's land I shall stand, up here, just me and my guitar. No electricity. No amplification. No flamethrower. Quiet inside without even the standing lamp we use during rehearsals. Vocals are pointless in a room like this. Aren't they? Being lead vocalist is a fool's errand. During the chorus of "Fuck Creation," Transformer is supposed to lean into the vacant spot where you might imagine a microphone and blast his harmony. As the one doing our sound, Spit better be ready for that.

While I'm going over these preparations in my head, Spit hurries back to the front to inform the band that Darren is standing along the wall.

"What's he doing here?" Transformer grimaces.

"Relax. He didn't bring his twelve-gauge."

"What?"

He's come in peace, she means.

I nod to Darren. In return, Darren waves and gestures to the rebels at his side. The Willeys and Nick are in attendance too.

Spit returns to the back of the room where Darren and his sidekicks are lined up and, from afar, gives us a thumb's up.

"Time to introduce us," Transformer says.

Why me? Why not him? I glance over at my brother frozen at the ready, foot about to plunge into his distortion pedal. I catch something else, that Transformer is grinning. That he's enjoying himself. And decide that it had better be—*why not me?*

144

"Hello," I say out loud, in a voice that is just a bit louder than my speaking voice. "Our name is Because."

No response.

We play a four-song set.

No encore.

No covers.

Covers are for cocks.

PRESENCE

After the show, Darren and Nick and the Willey twins depart without saying a word. Without congratulating us, without telling us we sucked.

We head to the bus stop. No Uncle Per for the ride home. Roadies are unreliable. Luckily there was no stage constructed for this tour, nothing in the shape of a starship to be dismantled after each show and packed into eighteen-wheelers.

Once we reach the back of the bus, Spit lays across the double seat, then right away pops up and sits upright.

"You guys need stage presence."

"Talk to the frontman," Transformer says.

"The songs came through," Spit says. "But when you addressed the audience, Hombre, we could hardly hear you."

Well, whose fault is that? Anyway, I didn't know what to say. It made zilch sense to be up there in the first place. Plus, no microphone.

"Excuses," Transformer says.

"Look at it this way," Spit says. "You need to put on a live show, precisely in these situations, when the audience is rowdy or hard to please. I've said before you need more presence."

"Stage presence," Transformer quips.

"How about him?"

"He's a handful. At least I could hear his guitar."

"But I didn't have my…"

"Excuses." Grinning, he is.

"Don't take it personally, Hombre. You can work on something before the next gig. Go see some concert movies. Have you guys seen *Gimme Shelter*?" Nope. "*The Great Rock 'n' Roll Swindle*?" Nope. "Just get out there more. You should go downtown and see some local bands."

"I'm not eighteen…" Obviously.

"He's just a baby," Transformer reminds everybody.

"I know the doorman at Station 10."

She would.

"I could sneak you in," Spit says.

"This is our stop," I say.

"Adios."

"Thanks for doing sound," Transformer says.

Time to get moving. We get up and haul our stuff to the front and, when the doors wheeze, we wave to Spit as the bus gets moving again.

EXCELLENT

Later that night, we're still buzzing. In our room without Spit around, Transformer comes on all "excellent" about everything.

"That was excellent. You played excellent, Hombre."

"Thanks."

"You introduced us and everything."

But no one heard a word.

"It was excellent. Did you see Sister Candy?"

Nope.

"She went nuts."

She didn't. Was I the only one to notice Candy wheel the Colonel to safety after we opened with "People Disease"? She never returned for the rest of our set. Four songs were all we had, and now I'm beginning to wonder if we overstayed our welcome. By the end, folks were playing cards and doing puzzles.

"You're not saying anything," Transformer says.

"I was just thinking."

"What about?"

"I was a bit scared."

"Same here. Forget about it. We'll get used to it." I hope so. I'm still recovering three hours later. Transformer kneels before the record player. "What do you want to hear?"

Music is the cure.

He puts on REM. The singer's voice is muffled. The guitarist doesn't bend notes. The bass rolls and the drums snap. I can't put my finger on it, but I like them more each time we listen to them. Him too. REM is growing on us, growing in the background. Last week, Spit showed me how to play this song by sliding my hand up the neck in the E Major position, how to get that full ring from the open strings. It's not a bad move.

Suddenly I pinpoint what's been on my mind. "Nobody reacted. They didn't even pretend to like us. It was like we hadn't played music to them."

"I noticed that too," Transformer says. "What did you expect for a first gig?"

Signs of life. Applause. Appreciation. At least smoke signals. And I expected feeling different inside afterwards, not just embarrassed.

"The vets are on lots of medications," Transformer says. "Remember what Candy told us. They're all on drugs. Some have lobotomies. The Colonel must have been Morfar's age. Anyway… it's the exposure that counts." Exposure? "And you heard Spit. Just a few complaints but that's typical of sound engineers. They set up the PA and everything's perfect—no buzz in the lines, nothing muddy between the soundboard and the microphones. Things are under control, airtight. Until the band shows up and ruins everything."

"There was no system! We didn't have a PA!"

"I'm joking." He throws the pillow that bonks me on the head. "Are you out of it or what?" I must be. "Do you know what I was just thinking? We should record an album. What are we waiting for? For the cover art, I want you to imagine you and me sitting on the roof with all these black birds perched on the headstock of my guitar."

"Why black?"

"Because white is for magicians and hippies. White doves mean peace. We'd get crows. Call the album Into the Ground." His call. "Into the Ground…" Transformer repeats the name aloud with more care. "Into the Ground. We'll do a demo and send copies to Megan at *The News and Chronicle* and to Lepage at *The Gazette*. Slowly build a profile. Then, for better exposure, open for a band coming into town…" I presume that means putting a stop to playing at hospitals, that sunrooms are passé. "You heard what Spit said. We get our stage show together and ride the wave with our following to the end of the line."

A following *plus* groupies is fertile stuff. Warm manure. A dream without bullshit will not grow. I get it. Tomorrow morning may come with a case of dreamer's remorse, but this won't be Transformer's last chance to lecture me about punk or copyright or to double down on his desire to sing a duet with Patti. We're just getting started.

DEAD LISTENER

Spit, let me tell you about my second act. I am busking. Remember Transformer once called it "begging with strings attached"? That about sums it up, this gig. I've been at it years. I wear my tight black trousers still, and smoke my own, rolled, but it ain't me, babe. It still ain't me. I used to dread this, dread becoming a pathetic figure, turning into one of those journeyman musicians who play a mean blues guitar and, for a half century, steadfastly force themselves upon the locals in tiny nightclubs across the city, never once giving anybody a goddamn break by getting out of town, even for a long weekend. No, not the local testament to stamina, the humble freak-show status enshrined by sheer doggedness, the gargoyle that conveys grotesque sentimentality and placates every passerby with a nostalgic soundtrack leading nowhere.

I'll admit, at first, I felt like a performing clown, an impersonator, anchoring my set with the finicky harmonic intro to "Roundabout" and wooing tourists with the spider-finger picking on "House of the Rising Sun." I've gotten away from that. I had to compile my set of crowd-pleasers, but I still sneak in personal favourites like "I'm in Love with a Girl." I mix it up from week to week. I switch out songs. But yeah, it still ain't me, babe! I'm not there. I never do originals. Nope, it isn't the old Hombre.

Playing covers is for losers, but I'm beginning to enjoy the gig. What does that say about me? My repertoire includes Big Star, REM, the Waterboys. Sprinkle in a few oddballs by Lloyd Cole and the Commotions, season with Joy Division, and there you have me facing down the street or standing in a station of the metro. For the especially down-and-out hard times, I pack my back pocket with Dylan and Neil Young, but all in all I don't exactly give the people what they want. I mean, Lloyd Cole? The old masters are printed money and I won't ever surrender them, but please, hear me out, dead listener: permission granted to liquidate my busking ectoplasm with intergalactic karma if ever I pull from my hat Barenaked Ladies or Blue Rodeo.

Why?

Because, trust me, they're fucking awful.

p.s. What music do dead people want to hear? For the record, tonight I busked my rendition of "Working Class Hero" on the corner of St. Laurent and Pine. That song breaks me up. I'm still a fucking peasant, as I am sure you've heard.

OF DEMOS AND DUMMOS

SCHOOL

Arriving back home after doing the route, climbing the stairs, opening the door—the room is hazy and the decibels deafening because the yogi sitting cross-legged between the house speakers is blasting the great album *Transformer*, his namesake.

"Pay attention and listen to this." He stabs an incense stick in the direction of the turntable—an instruction to me, his pupil.

This. Done-It-All-Lou. Listen to Lou. Lou, Lou. Lou: going on about things, things, things. And making the sour sweet. Spouting the indiscreet.

I've been to school and returned and delivered the papers, and in the meantime, Transformer hasn't left the house, hasn't left our room. All day, he's been hooked up to the stereo, transfusing Lou Reed's rough street poetry. Making this for him such a perfect day.

"Come, drop your purse and sit."

My purse? My purse is his purse. We carry the same forest-green army surplus bag. On a long thin strap, it hangs low to the hip. While he was stationed at Bethune, Transformer got teased for having what the jocks identified as his purse. The jocks and most other kids carried an Adidas bag and wore

Kodiaks, the standard issue for infantry. Last week, Transformer drained seven reservoirs of Wite-Out to label his bag with "Fuck Creation." I copied him and had my own labelled "Fuck Creation" until the powers that be at Bethune lectured me about how school prefects ought to set an example. I scratched out my early work and put "Cain is Able" as my calling card, which no one seemed to mind. Or understand.

Purse or no purse, I'm in no mood to follow his instructions today. The volume is giving me trouble seeing, as if my wires are crossed and my ears are borrowing power from my eyes. Instead of staying put and curling up inside the incubator, I bypass the yogi and go out onto the roof, and from up here, Flowers catches my eye as she raises her coffee cup.

"Do you want some?"

I do, I decide, and descend the ladder to join the house Swedes on the lawn.

"We've got late summer," Morfar says, his golf shoes' white tips peeping from the bottom of pressed grey wool pants.

"I love this time of year," Flowers says before she stands to offer Mormor the big plate of kaka.

"Tack," Mormor says and receives her second portion. "You too, you should eat," she urges me, gesturing to the cake. "Eat something."

"I will," I say.

"I *have to* keep eating," Mormor says, admitting failure, emitting her familiar body tremble of disgust. "Or else I'll turn out like a skeleton. Just wrinkles and bones."

A blanket is draped over her knees today. The torture it is for her to eat when she would rather keep her eyes closed for taking sun.

"The rest of the world is on a diet," Flowers says and hands me a big plate. "And my own mother force-feeds herself and complains about it, because it goes against her nature."

"A little is enough; the right amount is a feast," Morfar says, repeating the house mantra with a gentle smile.

"Lagom," Mormor says.

Morfar touches her knee. "Lagom," he testifies.

"Lagom är bäst," Flowers completes the phrase. This the folk law by which the Swedes live. Just the right amount is best. A little over and you're done for.

"What are you doing down there?" Transformer appears on the roof. "Aren't you coming back in?"

"Won't you come down?" Flowers pleads.

"We are having a feast," I say, raising my plate.

"I mean it." Transformer turns. No way he's joining little Europe. "Come in, Hombre, to do your homework."

BLAKE

"I lost Mum when I was six. And your Dad died at Expo? Your brother told me. He was two years old, and how old does that make you? Not yet born? There's your song of experience, kiddo."

I just sit in the chair across from him and wait for Mr. Dawson to finish.

"You've read Blake? You will. I bet all those colour-by-number poets of the curriculum don't need a text-pert expert, do they? But Blake. Blake will etch himself into your mind. *Songs of Innocence and of Experience*. Everybody has the same two sides. Side One is your edgy, paranoid, insecure side. Side Two is your sensitive better half awash in indolence. The two sides yearn for synthesis, don't they? Does any of this make sense to you?"

"I guess."

"I pegged you as smart. A prefect."

"It wasn't my choice."

"Song of experience right there."

Sure.

"There will come a day—a day when you'll be sitting in your room in Dorval listening to music with Transformer, and both sides will play for you at once, turning consciousness into the medium. That's what I call true stereo. High fidelity."

"I can't wait," I say, and then, emboldened, "I might need a note to get back into class. It's been over thirty minutes."

"To whom should I...?"

Whoever.

"We're taught revolution, not evolution." Back at home, Transformer has lots to say. Subjects like biology, chemistry, and math are frowned upon by him. Meanwhile, at Bethune, as he well knows, they push the sciences on us. Not Dawson but every other teacher.

"At New School, we're not forced to clone ourselves."

"Lucky for you," I say. "I really like English, except this month. This month we're bogged down in war poetry, but we get to read other stuff."

"Mr. Prufrock, I presume? Let us go and kiss the sky?"

Funny.

"English is English. English is fine," Transformer says, "but what about anarchy? Never mind the bollocks of Bethune. The real thing." He rolls up a sleeve. "Anarchy and art…" Rolls the other. "Art isn't about using coloured pencils. In theory, there are really two choices. Revolution or plagiarism."

I wonder how we got here. I was going to talk about Blake. About our two sides, about experience and innocence.

"We're reading Paul Gauguin's diary," he announces.

"Who?"

"Go-gain. The painter from France. He was wild."

"What did he paint?"

"Fruit trees, flowers, gourds."

Doesn't sound so wild.

"And all sorts of naked people."

"Did he ask them first?"

"For what?"

He scrapes at his scalp with his claw.

"Was he part of the French Revolution?"

"You don't get it." Huge sigh of aggravation from the number of the beast. If it's so important, he should explain what he means about Gauguin and the revolution. Instead, he's back to listing the merits of New School: anarchy, spares, revolution, and the possibility of him graduating without studying mitosis.

"Congratulations, but who cares?"

"I do," he says, like it's a matter of principle. If only we all could be sheltered from knowing about the reproductive cycle of lowlifes.

"New School suits my temperament," Transformer continues. "We don't waste our precious time dissecting rats or rainbows."

He's not been to school since Tuesday—he's been at home nursing a stomach ache and his big lie of silence. Still, Transformer could serve as New School's Minister of Bollocks if only he attended class more often. He's focused on becoming a truant. He stands by that word—truant—steadfastly. In Transformer's world, being a truant means you're some kind of truth-seeking anarchist.

"I've got some real homework today," I say.

"Not so fast," Transformer says and again jabs the incense stick in the direction of the turntable—*pay attention to this*. Last Thursday, the listening assignment was the Buzzcocks, and on Sunday morning we studied Talking Heads. Monday afternoon, Television squeezed around to the front of the class. While the teacher wasn't looking on Tuesday evening, Neil Young passed me a note. Today, in detention, for extra study after the Lou Reed pop quiz, Transformer blasts me with a bit of Joy Division. May we pay attention to this! Maintain sacred silence for the Manchester band's good lesson in jittery and haunted energy.

After Joy Division, I grab my guitar, and within seconds I'm playing a new riff on the bass strings. Transformer just sits there. Watching me. Like I'm Darren. Like I'm poison.

"What's wrong?"

"Plagiarism."

Get ready for extra study.

"Be yourself or become like everybody else. Revolution or plagiarism. Copy the old shit or make something new. I told you, Hombre. This is the good news. We're going to sound like you. Not them," he points to the turntable.

"I'll need your help," I say.

"You're the one came up with 'Fuck Creation!'" Not just me. Him too. "What do you think that's about?"

"I don't know."

"You don't know?"

Nobody ever asked me.

"You mean Megan from the *Chronicle* hasn't asked you, so you don't know yourself?"

He has it all figured out.

"Don't worry," Transformer says. "You come up with the

goods and we'll put the songs through the old Transformer before we send anything out into the world."

Sounds revolutionary.

DEMO

Spit is the engineer, Transformer the producer.

This is our first recording.

The very first.

Historic.

"What does the producer do?" I'm here for the asking.

"I make the most important decisions."

There's my answer. I'm just on rhythm and the singer in the band. The window is closed to reduce outside noise. The door is closed to keep any wandering Swedes out. The three of us are gathered in close at the desk, a makeshift altar upon which rest two microphones and the double cassette machine. It feels like we're prepared for a press conference, only without any press in attendance.

"Are you almost ready?" Spit asks.

"Not yet." The producer is changing his outfit at the last moment. He finds a sweatshirt, adjusts his headband, and then Transformer's down on the floor wriggling like a snake. It takes him an eternity to shed his jeans for an identical pair.

"You're such a girl," Spit says.

"You too," Transformer beckons, meaning I should change into something less comfortable as well.

"You better," Spit says. "Here, give me that." Spit relieves me of my guitar. "You can't play it like this anyway!" While she begins tuning, I go stand in the closet and turn my shirt inside out. I'm not Superman and I'm not looking like a Sex Pistol, but it's at least something.

"That's much better," Transformer says. "A little respect. History happens once. Trust me, you want to look the part."

"Sit down," Spit orders him. "What are we recording first?"

"'From This Room.'"

The song is a two-chord wonder. Transformer down-strums while I play variations of the chord, sliding up and down the neck, sounding the high strings, using the purple pedal for an underwater sound. If we play it right, the song comes to life and our band sounds complete without bass or drums.

"All right. I need to take levels." Where does she get this stuff—levels? As Spit reads the UV meter, the needle swings left and right.

"Sit back a bit." She motions for us to move our chairs further away from the microphone. Then we try again. She raises her hand. "That's perfect."

So here we go. This time for real. Jamming and rehears-ing, the risk is zero. This is different. This is unnatural. This is like volunteering to take a lie detector test when you know ahead of time you can only lie, or trick yourself, to get through it. We are crossing a line here. Transformer and I, with Spit by our side. She presses record.

"Take One."

Transformer says, "Wait." The tape keeps running. "Is that part of the song now? You talked."

"I'm supposed to," Spit says.

"Hmm."

She stops the machine. "Let's do it again. Ready?"

"Ready to die," he says.

"Me too." I'm nervous. In practice, I play my guitar part with a vengeance, a real edge, making the song ours by doing what nobody else can do. I'm eager to do that.

Spit punches the record button.

"Take One."

"Isn't it Take Two?" The words just come out.

"You ruined it."

Look who's talking.

"Relax," Spit says. "We have all day."

All day, and all of the night! The wheels turn again. Transformer starts down-strumming furiously, holy shit, hammering the intro. I hit my first notes clean and hard. We go another two rounds before Transformer begins to sing. The red light is eating us up. Together we've listened to a lot of songs on this tape machine—now it's as though the same machine is listening to us. I'm getting goosebumps. The first verse is my favourite. Concentrating on my playing at the same time, I've got chills. Here we go sending a signal out into the world that we're alive. With this song, we're coming out.

From this room, I can see the world
Blue and green, and it's black at night
From this time, I am going away
In this world, I cannot stay

After three minutes and thirty seconds, Spit motions for us to freeze. The dregs ring out, sweet vibrations until...
"That's a take," she says.

"Woof! Woof!"

Transformer jumps out of his seat! "Woof!" Barking like a dog. Did we catch it? Feels like it. I'm out of gas. Spit rewinds the tape. She presses play and we slump back against the wall on my bed, faces flushed, radiating with dreams of glory as we listen back to the band's first recording. Enthralled, we listen hard. We listen over to a recording that sounds and doesn't sound like us. We sound better than any of us thought possible.

"Great song!" Spit says.

"He wrote it," Transformer says.

"Not alone."

Everything is his and mine and his.

"Strong melody," Spit says.

Everything is ours.

"Hombre, your timing is a bit off," Spit says, "but you came up with a really great part."

"Thanks."

"Anyone can learn timing." Transformer comes to my defence, but he doesn't have to. I'm over the moon. She rewinds and we listen back again and again. Soon we have our first visitors knocking at the door. Flowers and Candy.

"Come in," Spit says.

"Is it safe?" Flowers says.

"Rush didn't have to put up with this," Transformer says.

"Oh shush." Flowers sits on the bed.

"Let's hear it," Candy says.

Spit rewinds the tape once more. "Here goes," she says, and when the first notes sound, Flowers jumps.

"Why do you sing in that voice?" Candy asks Transformer.

"That's my singing voice."

"I didn't know people had a singing voice," Flowers says. "What's a singing voice?"

"It's when he sings," I say.

"Well, I think it's very nice," Flowers says. "You'll have to play it for Mormor and Morfar. They've been waiting downstairs. I'm sure they would love to hear what you all have gotten up to."

"Sure," Transformer says. "If they're into Echo and the Bunnymen, this will be a dream for them."

"They're proud of you already."

Flowers gets up. Unconditional loving is done here.

"Are you all right?" Flowers says, noticing how my legs are quivering. I can't control them. All the twitching. And I still have goosebumps.

"He gets like that," Transformer says. "Matter is created and Hombre is destroyed. He'll recover."

GULAG

"Where's the fucking bus…" Transformer says, crouched low while making a fire and not expecting an answer from me, because there is no answer.

Waiting for the bus is a state of mind, a big waste of time. The 211 is the only bus that links Dorval to downtown, and it marches to the offbeat. The bus shelter is boredom's club-house. It's public property waiting to be destroyed. The shelter is a great place to practise donkey kicks; breaking physical things provides relief from pent-up frustration, for at least a little while, until the pressure of waiting for the bus builds again and this state-of-mind thing feels like it's going to ex-plode into something big and ugly. That's usually when the 211 appears, inching along the lakeshore on the far side of the bay like an earthworm minding its own blind business.

"Hombre, you can write your next song about it."

If I did write a song about the bus, I would include a winter verse with minus forty-degree winds driving across the lake. I'd describe how from inside the shelter you can't see much because the synthetic windows have been scratched and clawed into a dull cloudy haze by the degenerate animals who are forced to stand by for the arrival of an approaching rescue vehicle. For the times of insane cold, I'd preserve an image of

Transformer horking ferociously at the windowpane. In song, I might describe his gob freezing on contact and making a *tic* sound. This as proof that the entire band will die from hypothermia one of these days unless we get out of this gulag.

"This is just like Fart," Transformer says, tearing pages from *Hit Parader* before crumpling them into little balls and lighting them on fire.

"Pyro." I whack his butt.

"Here goes Sting," Transformer tosses him, the king.

"ELO!" I beg of him. Heeding my instructions for once, Transformer drops the cornballs into the flames.

All right. It's not that cold today. It's only October. But we're excited to be heading downtown and, at the same time, aggravated to the point of vandalism since we've been delayed by the prison system. We both remember Morfar's story about his days in the merchant marine when he sailed North Sea waters—how when the ship ran short of heating fuel, the sailors collected the shipping company's wood furniture to break it apart and stuffed the pieces into a barrel to light a bonfire on deck. Burning company property their act of defiance. But Morfar didn't tell it that way at all. What I grasped was the camaraderie among the seafarers. Their solidarity. Warmth. Yet I was struck by the melancholy in Morfar's eyes as though some clouding mists of those difficult days were trapped still behind his square-framed glasses.

"Good riddance!" I swing around and put my foot through the bottom wall to kick things off.

"Crazy man!" Transformer says.

Yes, I feel crazy. Psycho. I'm excited. We have a demo. We're going downtown to see a band. Finally. To celebrate, the two of us start doing our little dance, hopping around the fire: "There goes the Boomtown Rats!" Transformer drops the Rats into the fire. And around and around we go until I spot the bus worming its way along the far side of the bay.

"Better put it out," I say.

"Let them eat kaka!" Transformer proclaims, punching fists in the air, doing a high knee-raised jig, before stamping out the fire.

The door wheezes open, and the bus driver flicks cigarette ash onto the steps.

We troop in and take seats near the back. We ride, ride, ride and don't say a word to each other until the bus creeps to a halt at Pine Beach, the last stop before merging onto the highway and speeding downtown.

Spit gets on at Pine Beach and takes her sweet time walking to the back at first. But then she makes a run for it and uses the metal pole like a firefighter to slide down beside Transformer and insert herself on the bench seat opposite me. Immediately, they do that annoying thing where people seated too close to each other will squeeze even closer and knock butts before motioning each other to make room. But no one moves. Meanwhile, bums forgotten have kissed.

Cute. Transformer slips his arm around Spit and gives her a squeeze; in return, she blows fake kisses to her honey. They have this little routine, which is news.

From across the aisle, Spit at last turns to me.

"How are you, Hombre?"

An afterthought that burns.

"I see you boys brought your purses. Smart."

Transformer cold-stares me for a slow second. Back in

the Bethune days when he was teased, Transformer stopped attending class. Mom couldn't get him to go. He missed a month of school. He's still sensitive about it. Purse is our word. Not hers.

"Yup." I give my painted purse a pat.

"Did you come up with that yourself, Hombre?"

"I am able."

"You're self-assured."

"What?"

"Nothing." The bus changes lanes, and Spit checks over her shoulder just as we are passing the warehouses in Lachine. She turns back to face me. "Hey, shouldn't you spell that with a capital K?"

"It depends."

"On what?"

"On how you spell it."

"Snarky," she says. "It's pretty funny. Cain is Able. Sure you don't mean Abel? I mean, it works both ways."

Now she's confused me. Not for the first time. "Hang on to your brother, Transformer, he's got something. Remind me, how long have you been together?"

"Since the very beginning."

"Wise ass." Spit knuckle-punches Transformer on the shoulder. They start messing around for a bit, punching and pinching and saying "That hurts" when it doesn't, until Transformer jumps up and grabs the pole and slides down in the seat on the other side of Spit.

"What time is the show?" I ask, just to get them to stop fooling around.

"We have lots of time. Are you nervous?"

No dignified answer. "A bit."

"Don't worry. I'll get you in. Trust me, you're in a band. That's your ticket. Station 10 is small and loud. The stage is at the back near the toilets and the bar is along the wall…" As Spit begins laying it out for us, Transformer turns around to watch traffic out the window. He's listening but not listening. I'm taking in everything. Assimilating her every word into a vortex of daunting desire. Spit is telling us she knows the guy who does the door. "…but if you can't get in because he isn't there and the replacement bouncer is a dickhead, then we can go to the Moustache instead." I nod. In fact, plan B makes me feel a whole lot better because if "someone" isn't going to get in, that loser is going to be me, Hombre. At the same time, I badly want to see the Darned. Tonight! This band with the poet of a lead singer. This band with the tasty guitarist. This band I only know from Megan's review. Megan gave their single "Cigarette Jeans" four stars.

"…Moustache is a biker place. No preps. No punks. No disco trash. You'll see for yourself—if we go. The place is crammed with leatherheads plus rocker chicks with crazy tits. It's totally warped. The ladies have freaky orange suntans. The sun must keep them horny."

Or something. Horny or something. I've never thought of taking sun in that way. Across the aisle, Transformer takes up Spit's forearm and begins playing it gently like a guitar, delicately bending invisible strings, making the sweet notes weep. It's quite the moving performance. However, Spit has seen this act before, so she mostly ignores him and continues telling me about the Moustache.

"Bruce used to take me there."

"Who's Bruce?"

"Just some asshole I used to be with. Also he's a DJ."

"At the Moustache?"

"No! Not there. Bruce gets hired to do school dances. He brings in the sound system and the lights. His stupid record collection with Clapton and Deep Purple. He's probably done a Bethune dance. He did my school. That's how I met him. He's an asshole though."

"No kidding." Transformer fires his five cents.

"You don't even know him." Spit withdraws her fretboard arm. Transformer shrugs. He'll live to solo again. "Bruce got me in trouble… I'm not even allowed to go near him anymore. My brother Paul beat the shit out of him. It's a big mess. That's another thing about the Moustache—all the fights. Watch out for fist fights."

"Why?"

My balls are dust.

Transformer is nonplussed. He's reclaimed Spit's forearm to contribute an etch-a-sketch solo by her elbow.

"Don't worry. Mostly it just stinks." Spit squeezes her nostrils, in case we don't get it. "It's so loud that nothing feels real. Yeah, I did see this fight. Two bikers going ape shit. Ugly damage being done. They were going at it hard. But it's cool. They really care about things in there. They have their own set of laws."

Transformer is oblivious, twisting her forearm ever so slightly, feeling the fjords for a lost archipelago.

What she says drives electricity through my legs.

It leaves me jittery as the bus keeps rolling, speeding downtown.

THIRTEEN

When we get down at Station 10, I can see in it the doorman's eyes.

What's his age? The kid.

So we retreat.

I am almost fifteen and look almost fourteen and, in some ways, feel thirteen. Won't-you-let-me-walk-you-home-from-school thirteen. Won't you let me take you to the stupid school dance. That's what age I am.

Spit and Transformer put their faces to the front window, which bleeds a cardboard copy of the Darned.

"Can you see them?"

"Kind of."

Meanwhile, a group of kids start lining up at the door. I recognize Megan from the *Chronicle*. She's with this thin, tall blond guy who has a mature face, which makes him seem like he doesn't belong around here. Like he's famous but he's not. Like he's heard all the music there is to hear. I must be staring because, before going inside, Megan turns around and says, "Hi."

The group breaks into laughter as they cram through the entrance, but Megan turns again and stares at us before she disappears inside with her friends and the thin white duke.

"Who was that?" Spit asks.

"I don't know."

"Sure, you do," Transformer says. "Freckle face."

"Hombre has a girlfriend?"

"She's the reporter, Megan."

"How do you know her?" Spit asks.

"We don't."

"She recognized you?"

"She was being polite. That's all."

"Look at you, Hombre, starting to express yourself. You guys should send this Megan the demo. Anyway, news flash, girls are never only polite." Spit gets around to her point. "They're smarter than that."

Sure.

"She must have her eyes on you."

Sure. More like it must be her beat. Megan came to review the show. The show we're going to miss because I'm forever fucking too young.

MOUSTACHE

We about-turn and head west along Rue Sainte-Catherine towards this square across from the Forum on the corner of Atwater.

"During the day, this place is populated with winos," Spit says. Not at night. "Some people call it Pigeon Park." We walk along a path where the wood benches break on their own beachhead of breadcrumbs. The Forum, just across the street, is home to the Montreal Canadiens. As an NHL ice hockey rink, it doubles as the city's rock concert Mecca. This place called Pigeon Park is where the stoned lumberjacks assemble before entering the promised land by crossing the river Styx for a taste of Foreigner or Blue Oyster Cult. I've seen pictures of that kind of mayhem in the newspaper.

Alas, no concert tonight. We cut through the crowd of bleu, blanc, et rouge faithful, past the scalpers here and there who are selling the tickets they've thoughtfully kept tight to their bosoms—at triple the actual price. We head down a side street.

"Get ready. This is a real biker bar." Spit reminds us for the umpteenth time what to expect as we approach the entrance of the Moustache. There's no line-up, still the moose guarding the door impedes Transformer and me from gain-ing entry. He allows Spit through but holds us at bay be-hind his outstretched arm. Look who's in charge around here. Moose rubs ink into our hands. ADMISSION. We are stamped. Easier to find if he decides to slaughter us later.

"What's in your bag?"

"Nothing much."

He horks on the pavement.

"Let me see."

The remnants of a recent issue of *Hit Parader* get dug out from inside Transformer's purse. Not interested, he turns to me.

"What does that say?"

"It's stupid."

"Who's stupid?" Moose looms.

"Cain is Able. That's all it says... But it's dumb."

Moose squirts more juice onto the pavement. A group of bikers pass inside. We are cooked meat out here clutching our purses.

By this time, Spit comes back. "What's the hold-up? Give him a bill."

I'm as lost as Transformer.

"Give him something..."

I riffle through my things and come up with a five and our cassette, the band's first demo. Moose chucks the cas-sette into the road—and with a "Ladies," we are invited in.

The place is huge. Big showcase stage with track light-ing. It has the feel of a crowded mess hall with its dozens of wood tables. The four-man unit onstage is playing Sabbath. Covers are for cocks and for clowns, and bets are this place is packed to the rafters with both. It has the kind of dungeon atmosphere where it's safe to assume trespassers shall be kneecapped for a Police pin and flayed for wearing a Sex Pistols T-shirt. We wannabe punks are underage *and* undercover, which must be obvious to everyone in here. Instincts tell me to stick close to Spit. She's our ticket, our safety blanket.

"Look." Spit points to an empty table right in front of the stage. As we make our way through the bulging crowd, I'm keeping an eye on the lead singer, who is dressed in a cheetah vest and has jet-black hair and a jutting chin. The dude is wearing a leather neck-collar and a gas mask—the hard rubber ant-eater thing hanging from his belt keeps flipping around between his legs while he flits back and forth across the stage. Luckily for us, this cat is on a short leash: the chain connected to his studded neck collar is somehow anchored to the drum stand. But still, he gets out almost on top of the audience when he crouches at the edge of the stage and turns the microphone on the crowd and seemingly wills a rusty *I-Am-Ironnnnn-Man* from every croaking throat in the house. The man has presence.

Just as we get seated at the table, the drummer thrusts his arms into the air and, from behind his foliage of cymbals and toms, he displays wrists joined by handcuffs.

"Probably a good thing," Transformer quips.

The guy beside me knocks my shoulder. "Hey man, our friends had to leave…" and points to a half-full pitcher. "On the house." He grins and returns his attention to the girl at his side. None of us talk for a long while, not even Spit, which surprises me. She's gotten busy studying the guitarist's rack of pedals and gadgets. I have a broad look around the place and try not to show how out to sea I feel, while Transformer begins rapping his knuckles on the tabletop. Finally, Spit reaches for the pitcher and pours us each a glass of beer.

"I told you this place is wild," she says. "Cheers." And the three of us raise a glass just as the band launches into another song off *Paranoid*.

"Our uncle used to incubate to this." Transformer casually banters.

"Gross," Spit says.

"We have proof. Seen the art?"

Like it matters.

"The blurry guy holding a shield and a sword and the comets?"

"Yeah, that's it."

"Why *that*?"

Transformer shrugs. "People have different tastes."

"What about you? What's your favourite album?"

"*Horses*."

"Horses?"

"That's what I said."

"Patti Smith?"

"He wants to sing a duet with her." I perk up. "He made a bet…"

"She's so skinny," Spit says.

"I wonder why," Transformer says and raises an enigmatic eyebrow.

"How about you, Hombre?"

"Him, he's too busy." Transformer puts in a couple of good words for me: how I'm prolific, how I'm quiet. "He reads fancy books. He's a poet now."

"Come on, tell us your secret." She begins walking fingers

up my forearm and that's when I duck out. I hit some sloppy bumper-to-bumper traffic en route to the toilets but push through the fleshy masses, swaying to the wail of "War Pigs." All in all, I am feeling pretty good about this freedom. I am about to enter the men's through a saloon-style swing door. *Here you are, Hombre.* Bright lights ricochet off the white tile. *Don't forget this. You're downtown, you're coming along, you will do things tonight that...* Meanwhile, I come to and notice that I'm not alone: this blur of a girl is puking at the sink. She raises her head, touches her hair, and smiles at me in the mirror. Insane. Bladder. Pressure. But like this, I can't go. I count to ten under my breath. But nothing flows. She pulls down paper towels and hops onto the counter, shoves over beside me at the urinal. I stare at the wall. *The future is in your hands. For a good time, call Jeff.* Pubic hair sprouting from J-e-f-f. Nobody draws the erection and balls correctly, but even jocks can do a decent job with pubic hair because all you need is a bunch of squiggly lines.

Suddenly, she's bored and sighs.

"Sorry." Speaking to the floor. "That was gross. I puke a lot. I'm Julie." She wriggles her nose. "You got stage fright?"

"What?"

This girl Julie is swinging her legs just like she's at the playground.

"Do you think I'm pretty? Tell me the truth. I'm asking. Or do you think I'm boring?"

"No."

"You're not just saying that?"

Boring. Are you kidding?

"I knew you were nice the moment I saw you... My boyfriend's not nice."

When my bladder releases, she seems to lose interest and jumps down from the counter and starts banging on the door to one of the stalls.

"Hey, are you guys ever coming out of there? Come out!" Smoke rises above the stall, which signals to me that, whoever's in there, they've finished voting and there's a new pope in town. I quickly wash my hands. Upon leaving, Transformer bursts through the door and punches me on the shoulder. "Hi there, you're cute," Julie greets Transformer as I leave the scene.

Outside in the main room, there is a raging sea of noise. I do my best to walk a straight line back to the table, where I find Spit alone.

"These guys are ridiculous." Spit points at the band on-stage. Yeah. They are. Especially the grown man with curly black hair and the zebra-striped leotards. *But they can play*, I whisper, envious of the talent manifest in this monster player who seems at ease manhandling his lightning bolt–shaped guitar. While maniacally tapping hammer-ons, his strange hairy fingers work down the fretboard like scrambling rats.

Spit kicks my foot. "What's keeping Transformer?"

"Maybe he got lost."

This is a real possibility. We grin at each other. "Or maybe he met the love of his life." Could be. Spit kicks my foot under the table again. "Do you *like* anybody?"

Like and liking sounds infantile. In grade three, I liked my teacher. Before that, I liked climbing trees.

"Come on, you can tell me."

Not here, never. She grabs my wrist, changes tact: "What do you think the gas mask is for?"

"Maybe for when they go backstage."

"Yeah," she says. "These dudes must raise a little hell."

"Underarm hell." I kill the joke and we're back to watching the singer and the ugly man, rocking out, metal hair flailing, mirroring each other in a duel of the dumb.

"I bet you like Megan."

No reply.

"The newspaper girl."

Emotional rescue: Transformer returns, holding hands with Julie. Closer scrutiny reveals she's holding his hand, leading the way. It's child's play.

"What did I miss?"

"Your little brother here was just saying he thinks this band really rocks."

"You *are* brothers," Julie says in an excited way.

"Hi," Spit introduces herself.

"I'm Julie," Julie says.

"Yeah, but these guys are rip-offs." Transformer remarks about the crew onstage, acting the part of the new sheriff in guitar-town. "It's always the same with these hair lords."

"My brother Paul is into this stuff," Spit says.

"Iron Halen and Van Maiden," Transformer says, but not too loud.

"Motörhead. Sabbath. Zeppelin. Especially Led Zep. Page is a genius," says Spit.

Transformer begins soloing on Julie's forearm.

"That tickles," Julie says.

He stops, while a few other players at neighbouring tables go on riffing. Air guitar is popular in here.

"You can keep going," Julie says, proffering her arm like

royalty, a puke-bag princess.

"Zeppelin's early music is huge." Spit isn't done. "Have you seen them in concert?"

I bet nobody has.

"In the times of our youth, we must learn what it takes to be a man." Transformer sounds all sour about it, but holy crook, he's quoting from the Bible.

"That's not it!" Julie bellows. "'In the days of our youth, we are taught what it *means* to be a man.'"

"It's not a court of law," Transformer says.

"Lyrics are important." Spit says.

"Zep's done."

"They are *not*!" Spit and Julie are outraged. "Asshole!" Julie motions as though to break the air guitar over his head.

"Last year was such a sad year," Spit says. "First we lost Bonham, then Lennon gets shot."

"I remember that so well," Julie says.

Who doesn't? Lennon's crushed spectacles, lying on the pavement outside the Dakota. And the next day on the bus on their way to school, grade sevens are using Dakota in a sentence, casually, as if they hang together on the Upper West Side on weekends. As if they could find New York City on a map.

"In September we lost Bonham, in December John Lennon: Merry Christmas. I hope it's a good one!" Transformer sings a song.

Spit looks spooked. "Are you okay?"

"Perfectly," Transformer says.

There is without a doubt an uncomfortable silence, even though the place is rocking. Julie cautiously takes hold of Transformer's hand.

"I had tickets to their final concert at the Forum," Spit says, more downcast. "My boyfriend Bruce had a pair. Then Bonzo chokes on his own vomit."

People love to repeat that: Bonham choked on *his own* vomit. Like how klutzy. No one chokes on someone else's vomit, do they?

Julie says, "That's so sad."

Spit says, "It was the worst."

Julie asks, "Is Bruce still your boyfriend?"

Spit replies, "Not anymore."

I say, "He's a DJ."

"Who cares?" Transformer says and returns to his thesis on Led Zep. "Who is the genius player now? Les Paul Page? I doubt it. The man is heavily into Wicca." Transformer is bull-shitting-on-empty but still holds our attention. "The shit is always the same with these guys… It's a form of auto-plagia-rism… In our band, we're doing something different…"

That's a relief and reassuring to me to hear Transform-er say this about playing our own music, because I couldn't play any of the plagiarized shit he's been talking about if I tried, not after taking lessons from a witch.

"Hombre here is becoming a bit of a country boy. Aren't you, CB?"

They all look at me: Spit, Julie, Transformer. "His new songs have a fresh slant," Transformer says.

"I don't know…"

"What? Are you in a band?" Julie's eyes enlarge. "All of you?"

"They *think* they're in a band."

"What's the name?"

"Because."

"That's a funny name," Julie says.

"So is CB," Spit says. "Since when did you change, Hombre?"

Four days ago. By appointment of the sheriff.

"The rural runs deep inside my brother." Transformer raises his glass to make a toast.

"You're a real country boy," Spit says. "I didn't know that."

"You guys are fun!" Julie is impressed.

"Wait 'til you see their live show." Spit winks at me, the country boy from across the table.

"Oh yeah?" Julie is hooked. Her arm is looped through Transformer's and she's pulling him closer to her side.

"I've been thinking about the next show," Spit says, "and next steps, about your next move. I have this idea…"

"Shoot," says the sheriff.

"Just busk."

Just busk.

"What does that mean?" Julie the curious.

"It means you play on the street."

"That's what busking means?" Julie the befuddled.

"You put a hat down in front of you and play for tips."

"A beggar with strings attached," Transformer says.

"You're so funny." Julie tugs at him.

"The street is probably the best place to learn your chops. Think of all the people who might walk by in three hours, maybe two hundred?"

"If you busk downtown, you'll get thousands!" Julie's two cents.

"Our last gig didn't pay anyway." Transformer is coming around to the idea.

"I'll come and watch." Julie, his biggest fan. "And I'll bring people."

"Me too," Spit says. "I'll come watch."

"You can do our sound again." Is Transformer serious? "What do you think, Country Boy? We can hit Dorval Shopping Centre first."

Next stop, Fairview Shopping Mall.

"That's perfect." Spit is encouraged by how the tour is shaping up. "You can set up outside the music store." She means Brian's Music Store.

Transformer yawns. "Busking might be the way to go. We can push the record. Make some sales."

"What record?" I say.

"You know what I mean."

"You guys are so funny."

Spit checks her watch.

"Where do you live anyway?" Julie inquires.

"In a wasteland," Transformer says.

He means in the West Island. Last bus in fifteen minutes.

BEGGARS

Here goes nothing. We're bringing it to the streets. We set up in an area under the sign for Brian's Music Store. I'm not confident that busking off Carson Avenue is going to usher in street credibility. In this spot, we are likely to get routine afternoon traffic from shoppers leaving the Steinberg's grocery and others leaving the mall after a visit to the new pet store called Kittens. Out here, the sparkling parking lot is oozing black oil, and it smells like summer still. The pavement comes right in like a tide and surrounds the raised sidewalk we are using for our stage, which means that people getting in and out of their cars are going to be treated to a concert.

"Sorry I didn't bring people," Julie says.

"That's okay," I say.

"People never bring people," Transformer says, and he's probably right.

"When are you going to start?" Julie inquires, from the standing area upfront, already tapping her foot on the sidewalk.

"Anytime," I say. Same as the last gig. Nobody cares one way or the other. This is not like the Moustache, where hordes of horny bikers expect the presentation of well-baked covers on the double. This is our boring gulag. Anything goes.

"Hold on," Transformer says and gets busy fixing his hair while Spit knocks on the window from inside the store, where she is stationed with her brother Paul. I seriously doubt Spit will be able to hear us from inside. Could be that's the whole point. I reposition my guitar strap and feel for the harmonica, snug in my back pocket, remembering Transformer's fair warning that he'll break my teeth "if you blow that thing…" I won't blow it. But I have a right to carry it.

"What are you waiting for?"

Now we have Spit pestering us through the door.

"Nothing," I say, and out of the blue, Transformer launches into the opening riff of "Johnny Worm." The song about a pusher man. Who's pushing it now? Him, Transformer slouching in a tattered T-shirt with molested hair. Him, with a ruthless grip on the neck of his guitar. Him, strangling the opening notes. There was no count in, and now there's no room for me to come in. It's just him. Transformer: dismantling the prelude, tearing the melody apart note by note, roaring through the eruption of song until he's down to some last sniffs of crying feedback, which the fascist snuffs out by daubing the strings with his forearm.

"Holy shit, Transformer!" Julie is *super impressed*. She's jumping hard.

Before we know it, the first set is in the bag.

A blur.

Take five, ciggy break. Transformer strikes a match and ducks into the flame, which is when Flowers happens by pushing a shopping cart, with Morfar in tow, clicking right along in his golf shoes.

"Tell them we're on a break," Transformer whispers,

since it's below him to address the riff-raff.

"I'm impressed." Flowers smiles. "When do you go back on?"

"In about five," I respond.

"Hello, boys." Morfar stands up close, tap-dancing on the sidewalk cement. He's got a tremor. His own sweet vibrations.

"Hello, Morfar," I greet him. "How are you feeling today?"

I see he's cut himself shaving.

"Just fine," he says.

"This is our Morfar," I say to Julie.

"What does that mean?"

Never mind. Isn't it obvious? Julie goes inside the store to join Spit and Paul. The three watch side by side from the window. Paul has bulky shoulders and a moustache. Looks like a real Burton Cummings in his jean jacket with a lamb's-wool collar. He's only something like five years older than us, but he comes from a different era. Probably hangs at the Mapes with Uncle Per.

"We'll wait," Flowers says. "Take your rest time if you need it."

"We're not tired," I say. "Some bands play two-hour sets. And do encores. We only played twelve minutes."

"Take all the time you need," Flowers repeats, reaching into the shopping cart. "I brought you some figs."

"That's just great," Transformer mutters. "Now would you buzz off?"

This is when our sound technician steps outdoors and braves a word. "Mrs. Lindstrom, you are kind of in the way.

Your sons are trying to put on a show here."

"Is that so?" Flowers says, hands grasping the bar on the shopping cart.

"Sorry," I say. "She didn't mean to be rude."

"No need to apologize," Flowers says.

"Take your time, boys." Morfar pours unconditional love into the wound.

"Remember: presence," Spit says in my direction as I ready myself. "Feel your real self when you're up there."

"How?"

"Eat more," Transformer says.

"Look who's talking," Spit says.

"You should both eat more," Flowers says. She's been eavesdropping stage left. We are about to begin the second set when along comes Chris Burns—this kid I recognize from an article in the paper—the nose of his black guitar case bobbing up and down like a horse. Chris stops for a listen, although it's not his bag. His band is Terminal Sunglasses. He's young but looks older than me. Spit talks big about his playing. His hands. His fingers. The things he can do. He has a reputation. He's that rare technician with a punk attitude.

Morfar acknowledges Chris Burns by vaguely pointing towards his grandchildren: *Watch these guys.* Chris cracks a smile.

Fig, his presence makes me nervous. But at least we have a crowd forming. Chris Burns and Spit and Julie and Flowers and Morfar. Paul through the window. This time, Transformer counts us in. We launch into the second set, and right when we get going, Chris raises one hand to his chin and leans a bit sideways. It's as though he can't listen to music standing straight. Listening to music draws him off-balance until he's holding up a tower of awkward consideration.

"That's cool," Chris says before he leaves on his guitar horse.

Mugs of milky tea in the fall. I sneak them past the Swedes and up the stairs into our room. Milk tea comfort, a counterpoint to dead leaves and cold weather.

Thursday, and it's Transformer's week to deliver the newspaper, but the truant's been nailed to his bed all day. I am about to open my mouth and complain to him about busking—the pressure I felt to give the people what they want, to play the old masters and cover our asses in corny glory—when Transformer opens his mouth first.

"You've been spying on me."

"What are you talking about?"

"You know. Spying."

I settle the mugs down on the desk. He's not interested in my cloudy liquid offering.

"Hombre, we share the same room. Live almost the same life. You copy everything I do. And I find this." He flashes a notebook. "It's news to me—you exhibit an inclination towards the metaphysical."

"I do?" Couldn't care less. He's bullshitting.

"You do."

"If you say so."

"No, Hombre—you say so." Transformer sits on the

edge of his bed. "I read your diary. I'm not making any of this up."

"You *read it*?"

"The point is you've been spying and saying things about me."

Asshole. "It's private." It's mine. Not spying. I haven't been spying. In days gone by, the words "you're spying on me" were cause for a fight. It was this big capital crime if you got caught spying, even if spying is a childish game. It means you hide away to watch the other person. It's nothing. But after getting "spied on," you had the right to feel violated. Transformer and I signed a truce long ago, and for years we have only spied on Candy and Flowers. Spying is infantile, yeah, but it's real enough.

Transformer props the diary open on his knee and begins reading aloud.

I want to learn harmonica. Transformer says no. Not a chance. He thinks I should concentrate on guitar. He's probably right.

"There's more…" He flips forward. Of course, there's more. Lots more. I write in it at school so he can't see. I don't print dates. The pages are covered in this foreign handwriting: a tiny scrawl, letters scrunched, words wadded into balls. Glyphs hiding things too private for the light of day.

"Did you read it all?"

"Are you kidding? I skipped the part about you learning to tie your shoelaces—in fact, most everything from about age three to thirteen."

Funny.

Transformer turns the page.

*You won't ever hear what we hear. Music is our pledge!
You can eavesdrop (eh, Flowers and Candy?) but you
won't hear the real stuff.*

"When did you write this?" He waves the diary in my
face.

"Give it—"

The song we play is not the music we hear first.

Transformer clears his throat. "I really like this part…

*Are songs just like fossils underground waiting to be
discovered and brushed off and lifted from the earth?
Do we find songs, or do they find us? Are they physical or metaphysical?*

Sincerity is my curse. I want to damage him.

"Newton's first law, remember. Matter is neither created nor destroyed. Where does that leave you, Hombre, my
brother metaphysical?"

"Nowhere."

Transformer slides the diary across the floor. "Take it
back. But just so you know…" He pulls a pencil from behind
his ear. "…I made my changes."

"You made what?"

"Calm down."

He made changes to my diary. It's mine, my diary, not his. It's not the diary of a shitty painter from France who paints a gourd and gets to say stupid things about revolution… It's not his homework, part of his reading for New School. Can't he tell the difference? He's erased parts and put himself on the page as if Transformer is Hombre and Hombre is Transformer.

> ~~I did not know I had in me~~. *Song writing is exciting. The chords and words can take you ~~away~~ to a different place. I become the caretaker of the song. You just want to leave the beautiful thing be but at the same time you want to remember how to play it and the way you felt the first time you played it, which is almost impossible to do.*

Then in Transformer's own handwriting:

> *Writing a new song is, in my humble opinion, just an honest attempt to recapture that original flash, that first glimpse of inspiration, when the song was incomplete and incoherent and just damn perfect. The notion of the well-crafted song is therefore an oxymoron since the more "crafted" a song is the further it has strayed from that first moment of inspiration. Every song is a failed attempt to recapture the moment of inspiration.*

And this:

All songs are what you can express in the form that it is expressed in. That's about as slim as I can put it.

After reading, I take a long gulp of tea. "Who do you think you are? People don't do things like this."

"I'm not people."

No, he's not people.

"Don't get puritanical, Hombre. I'm your brother."

"Why doesn't my brother do the paper route? It's his turn."

"Turns and taking turns is for babies," he says like a baby and drags a baby's hand through his messy hair and sighs heavily like it's him, Transformer, who's been defiled and not me, Hombre.

"Anyway, I quit."

"You can't."

"I did already. Last week."

"Without telling anybody."

"Lighten up. Put something on," Transformer says, meaning he'd like to call a truce and listen to music instead of bickering. But I'm not in the mood. I'm not interested in another transfusion of Lou Reed or Talking Heads.

Sitting at the desk with my back turned to him, I light an incense stick. I blow on the tip, get it glowing.

"Hey, there's a party this weekend," Transformer says, changing the subject. "We should go."

I tear a page from my diary and feed it to the incense. The tip burns a bright orange, the corner of the page burns black and curls.

"I mean it, we should go. What are you doing?"

Nothing.

"Are you listening to me?"

Nope.

"Are you being a pyro?"

Nope.

"Hombre. Are you listening to me?"

Nope.

"Lawrence of Arabia was a pyro."

Ha.

"I'm not going to apologize."

I know that.

"Don't wait for an apology."

I don't trust him. "So you didn't read it all?"

"I said I didn't. Do you want me to 'promise'?"

I can't trust him. "I'm going." I run down the stairs and out the back door of the house and open the gate and jog down the road to the lakefront, where I try lighting the diary on fire with a match, but the wind is too strong. Why bother. I throw it far out and imagine it sinking to the bottom of Lake Saint Louis with the parts that Transformer said he didn't read still safe.

Although I know he read it all.

News gets around even when we don't deliver it door to door. At the kitchen table, Flowers speaks first.

"Boys, I understand that you're busy with the band. But I don't like what I've heard."

Flowers looks searchingly at me but should be focusing her attention on the truant.

"We all have to keep jobs and work." Candy lays down her view of the law.

"For how long?" Stupid question, but I don't want to hear Transformer's voice this early in the morning. I'm asking Flowers.

Candy responds: "She's not a fortune teller."

No, she's a bank teller. A bank teller who's planting the palms of both her hands on the surface of the table and begins a motion like smoothing out wrinkles in the wood.

"It's not a question of how long. I'd like you to learn to keep a job. It's simple as that."

"It's the damn principle, in other words." Transformer can't help himself.

"Shut up," Candy says.

"Hello, boys," Morfar says with a surprised ring to his voice after entering. "You're up early this morning."

Candy pours him a coffee, as Flowers is still massaging the wood tabletop.

"Tack."

"Let me tell you something. Your own Morfar…" Flowers is going to talk about Morfar in the third person with him present in the room, which is awkward. "At your age, he had already left home, worked on the freighters and eventually left Sweden for America and arrived in New York, where he became a tutor for two boys in a wealthy family. Isn't that right?"

Morfar accepts this version and nods to the music of time as Flowers repeats the familiar beats of the story—him teaching tennis and golf at a country club on Long Island before leaving the east coast for California to find work on the fruit farms and eventually getting into sales and becoming Vice President of Electrolux. The point of the story is my grandfather worked at something his entire life.

"And after he retired, he kept working! He started selling ionizers door to door. He quit when his legs gave out."

My only previous job experience harks back to the years when the family had a rust-coloured mutt named Jolly. Transformer and I were recruited for a backyard work detail called Shit Patrol. On occasion, Morfar would ride shotgun even if Shit Patrol was a two-person job: we headed out into the yard, me holding the garbage bag, Transformer using a shovel to do the heavy lifting. The stench made him gag, so he covered his face with a bandana. Sometimes I wore one too. Flowers paid us a good allowance for Shit Patrol. In those days, Candy called us the Poo Bandits because, at something like fifty cents a turd, she felt we were getting away with highway robbery.

"What if we want to work somewhere else?" Transformer says.

"Doing what?" Candy says.

"I'm not asking you," Transformer says.

"Well, you can't just quit."

"Candy is right," Flowers says. "Please don't quit."

"Well, you can't force me," Transformer says, sixteen going on thirteen.

Candy says, "Do you think I like my job?"

"That's not my business. And I don't care."

"Wake up. Do you think working at the bank is a dream job for mom?" Candy says. "Counting other people's money?"

At the mention of money, Morfar gets up from the table, pushes his chair back in, and leaves.

"Five days a week. She does it for the family. For everybody here."

"You forgot to say she does it for the money."

"Child."

"There's no need to get nasty—both of you." Flowers reaches out to grab both Candy and Transformer by the wrists. That's her only form of punishment. Squeezing your wrist.

"I'll still do it," I say to make Transformer and Candy stop fighting.

"You always do that," Candy says.

"What?"

"Apologize for him."

I guess so. Flowers lets go. Meeting adjourned.

ROOSTER

He's been gone, gone so long. Out collecting. I deliver, Transformer collects. That's the new arrangement.

"How can you listen to this, Hombre?"

Shrug.

"Turn it off. Mick Jagger's a freak."

Right.

"You like to suffer?"

Sometimes. But it's not about that. Transformer empties his pockets of small change.

"Lots of tips?"

He ignores me, dances the cocky rooster in front of his Patti Smith poster. "Nothing from the houses in Valois. Only a quarter each from the apartments."

He pouts, then gets straight into bed without undressing.

"What's wrong? I'll change the music."

"No, leave it," he says.

"It's early," I say.

Only eight o'clock.

"I don't feel good."

He's lying on his side facing my side of the room.

"Are you sick?"

"I just told you. I don't feel good."

"You were just dancing."

"I know I was."

"I'll turn it down."

"It doesn't matter."

His face doesn't move when he talks.

"I kind of like it," he says.

"You do?"

Transformer turns to face the wall. This rooster needs his sleep.

12:45 a.m. on the digital-clock radio. A faint red glow spills onto my pillow. While Transformer sleeps, I cut away to an image of Mr. Dawson leaning back in his swivel chair, speaking like an oracle, riffing on music and religion, repeating the things that swim in my head.

"Listen up. Groupies began with Jesus. His twelve apostles. Twelve good men. Groupies are significant, more crucial than a record deal. They are sustenance. They'll come to the shows. They'll copy the early recordings and pass them around. Trust me, these sorts will blow your mind. If you get lucky, your groupies will form a movement and dedicate the rest of their lives to bringing your music to world consciousness. Shit, it's like socialism or communism. Because everybody wants to change the world. Because! That is not bad for a name for a band. Is it pure stoicism? What drives you?"

His questions are not questions.

"Who are you listening to? Sex Pistols? What about your brother? The Stranglers? The Psychedelic Furs? Ramones? The Beatles are choirboys in contrast, real charmers. Your brother's hero, Lennon, was a self-declared genius from the sticks. Lennon's muse was raw emotion and pain."

The more Mr. Dawson talks, the more he ties Transformer into everything. He sometimes talks like he's a member of our family.

"The oracle from Merseyside had a boner for rock 'n' roll. He had yank worship. He was a hippie. Same as Jesus. I mean, look at pictures. I heard your father was a bit of a hippie too. I bet your parents carried a membership card to the Age of Aquarius. Paid dues in loincloths and plants. I was a hippie, too, in my day. If you had long hair, smoked dope, were unemployed, liked rock 'n' roll, and you liked to make love outdoors, then we're talking about being a hippie. 'Make Love, Not War.' 'Give Peace a Chance.' All the songs of innocence. Being an artist is to be a believer. Boy, believe that what happens to you is of interest to the rest of fucking humanity. How does that land?"

12:55 a.m. on the digital-clock radio. A faint red glow spills onto my pillow. While Transformer sleeps, Mr. Dawson's bollocks swim in my head.

DUMMOS

Enter the ghost in the machine. Enter the four-track, the Fostex: this black-and-orange box with dials and sliders.

It gets the Transformer crowing. "This is a step up. How long can we keep it?"

"The weekend. Enough time to complete a real demo." Spit has it on loan from Paul, who swiped it from the music store, under his boss Bruce's nose. It's semi-stolen goods.

"Good work." Transformer relieves Spit of the four-track and places it down on the desk, stands off a few paces, regards it like a meteorite.

"How many microphones?" I ask.

"Two." Spit holds up one in each hand. Thin and tubular. Without round heads, these things look like sticks of dynamite.

Spit begins a walkabout of our room, inspecting all four corners as if she's never visited the place before and is seeing it through new eyes. She mumbles stuff about click tracks and ping-pong and fade-outs. "Can we take that down?" The poster of Bjorno de Borgerac? No chance. What's she thinking? She peeks inside our closet behind the mirror, a space that extends deep into a lost dimension: I used to crawl inside to the back where the floor is covered with untinned tennis balls and loose pieces from board games and hockey cards. I'd sit there, a matter-of-fact six-year-old in the pitch black, and call what I was doing hiding. My hiding. I once found a key jammed between floorboards and studied its puzzle-cut blade by running my finger across its ridge, exploring it like Braille. Another time, in a circus act worthy of grade six, I scrunched over and tried to lick my own pieces. I'm still surprised at myself.

"Perfect," Spit says, taking a final glance into the closet. "This will do for a dead chamber." She turns to face Transformer. "We can put you in here to record the guitar, and we can try background vocals from inside too."

"No chance. You can put Hombre in there."

He's not having it. Not having any special effects if it means him crouching inside with the door closed. But why not try? I'm getting excited. Who knows? Years from now, all those Because groupies might buy copies of *Creem* to find out how we got our Dorval sound. Then again, the closed closet might reproduce the effect of a suffocating box. A dead chamber, yes. For the musicians and sound.

"I'll come back tomorrow," our chipper sound engineer quips, "and we'll get an early start."

"See you at noon…" Transformer feigns a yawn.

Spit departs, leaving us the rest of the afternoon and the entire evening to ponder the Fostex. My adrenaline runs wild just looking at it.

"I'm wired," I say.

"You look it," Transformer says. "What do you want to do?"

We're out of sorts. It's impossible to relax with the four-track lying prone in our midst. Could it be spying on us? In a way that doesn't make sense, it is. Spying on us. Transformer begins making a list of the songs we should record over the weekend. His favourites. After pondering a bit, he drums the pencil on the tip of his chin.

"What should we call these sessions?"

"I don't know."

"Think."

"What about Demo Session II?" I suggest.

"You trying to make us laughing stocks? I'm thinking something like Dummy Sessions. Get it? *Now Presenting Dummy Sessions…*"

I'm probably the only person in the world who would get that and appreciate that his Dummy Sessions has the ring of an old-time comedian. Kind of.

"The Dorval Demos?" I put forward an alternative.

"Yeah right, Dorval is up there with Budokan. Let's stick with Dummy or what about Dummos?"

Dummos—punk for demos?

"The Dorval Dummos… or maybe… Because with Guests."

"What kind of guests?"

"Musical guests… like Spit."

"She's not a guest," I say.

"She can be," he says. "She can play bass as a guest star. We've talked about this before." Not really. We haven't. Though I wouldn't mind it. Bass is warm. Bass will fatten us up. Tie us together. That's what bass does.

COPYRIGHT

While we Dummos are still enjoying the comic potential of one Master Dummy Sessions, Candy knocks.

"You've got mail."

She shoves her arm through, and I slip out of bed and swipe the envelope from her hand.

"Thanks for coming up," I call through the door.

"That's okay, Hombre." Her soft footsteps descend back down the stairs.

"Put that away," Transformer says.

We've been getting mail—ever since Transformer read a piece about the perils of copyright theft in *Hit Parader.* Perils, yes, but it turns out copyrighting is a cinch and any dummy with a tape player can do it: you record onto a cassette and slip your crappy recording inside a self-addressed envelope and mail it back to our own address. Copyright is witchcraft.

"What's the use?" I questioned the vet several weeks ago when this sorcery just got started. We had gone for a walk down to the end of the street, where Transformer placed the first envelope in the mailbox.

"Don't worry. It's a genius system. We'll get it back in a day or two. The date stamp is our proof. No need for lawyers."

Then only a few days later, I returned home from school to discover Transformer listening to our first crap recording of "People Disease."

"What are you doing?"

"What does it look like I'm doing?" Transformer jabs a finger into the air. "You're off—right—here."

"You're breaking copyright." By opening the envelope.

"Listen to this next passage. You're off here, too, during the bridge."

"You weren't supposed to open it."

"Says who?"

Says he who makes the rules and breaks the rules. And what if I opened even one envelope?

"You wouldn't have, Hombre."

He'd have lopped off my ear.

"Not in your life."

For what it's worth, Transformer is right. I wouldn't open even one envelope. By now, there should be eight stuffed envelopes on the shelf because we have eight copyrights. I only see three. I place this next one beside the others to make it four.

ANTARCTICA

To record or not to record, that is the question. There won't be time to record them all. Those we record shall live. And any song we don't record today will die from exposure. Be swept aside. That's show business.

"Let's start with 'Grey Weather,'" thus decides the producer of our previous work.

"Grey Weather." Spit confirms. "Good. Let's get started." We record our guitars onto a single track first. Spit's bass on track two. Lead vocals on track three and harmony on four. It's a four-chord song and we're done recording "Grey Weather" in under an hour. The second song is just as easy. Same arrangements. Done in thirty. Then, in preparation for the vocal track on "Almost Happy," Spit positions Transformer in the closet. This one is not so easy. From behind the closed door comes the producer's lament: "I'm not happy about this…"

Too bad.

By strange magic, she gets Transformer to redo the singing of the chorus three times. "I'm almost happy! … I'm almost happy! … I'm almost happy!" He keeps at it longer than expected or I would have thought possible—until out he stumbles, face sweating and cheeks puffed red, at which point Spit signals for the band to take five and we dummos exit the studio one by one through the window for a ciggy break on the roof.

Outside, no one talks. It's awkward silence. Silence choked through smoke rings. We are devoted, reverent. Too serious and focused on the promised land of a new demo to make small talk. We need to keep in the groove and in this serious mood. A row of cars is backed up at the Stop sign. They must be following a detour. Our road is the first turn at the base of the overpass.

"Time to go back in," Spit says after passing the communal ciggy back around to Transformer, who casually drops the butt and watches it roll off the roof.

"Light show," Transformer says, giving the driver of a Mercedes a finger salute. Why, I don't know. There are no fluttering sparks this time as lit butt falls through the afternoon air and lands softly in the grass.

Back inside, it's time to tune up again before we attempt my new one called "In the House."

"I won't play on this one," Spit says. "It's too personal. Hombre, I'll record you live," she says, and surely by this she means she intends to record my vocals and electric guitar in one take. But the expression sounds strange, like I'm going to be part of an animal experiment—recorded live in situ, and as engineer she'll be able to dissect me.

"You can do it," Spit says.

"You're a regular Sting," Transformer says.

"I don't even play bass," I say.

"We know," Spit says.

"Shut up and play the song," Transformer says.

After six takes, I climb out of the hot seat.

"That was magic," Spit says.

Thank goodness, because my nerves are shot. We've done a solid five songs, and I feel rubbery. Transformer looks zonked. But the Fostex beckons. It demands our attention, and with the energy left in the tank, we're willing to try anything.

"I have a song," Spit volunteers.

"Let's do it," Transformer says.

"Warning. It has no ending."

"That doesn't matter," Transformer says.

"What's it called?" I ask.

"Antarctica. It goes like this."

We listen to her play one round and then click into action. Transformer jumps on bass, and I begin hammering two notes while Spit sings the first verse. This is the first time I've heard her sing. In our room. Her own song. Nobody is reacting to this. Her voice is sinking me. It's something else.

"What are you staring at?" Spit asks.

"Nothing," I say.

"He likes your face," Transformer says.

"Jesus."

"It's a natural," says Transformer. "Let's try your song again."

For the first time ever, Spit looks worried.

"Come on," Transformer says. "Don't be a stupid technician about it…"

"I'm not," she says. "Okay. If you really want to."

I can't hide my smile.

"What are you smiling at, Hombre?"

Everything.

"For the ending," Spit says, "everybody hold on a D and keep playing it over and over and over."

"Got it," I say.

"For as long as you can, keep it steady. Don't change chords. Keep plugging away on D and I'll fade it out later."

"Fix it in the mix!" Transformer says. "Studio magic!"

We go with it. Spit sings the first two verses before leading us into the chorus. "Antarctica. Antarctica. Antarctica." Performing impromptu like this is a thrill. "Antarctica. Antarctica. Antarctica." These are about the only words of the song. At last, Spit signals that we're coming to the last verse… followed by a final double chorus… and then… and now… easy… easy… hold on… Spit finds her D chord in the first position while I hammer on the fifth fret and Transformer thuds on bass: we're driving, grinding, turning the root over until it begins to feel like we could go on like this a long time… forever… spellbound, we've left the room… we're moving on from the neighbourhood… hitting asphalt… the highway… we're free as long as we can just hold this together.

DEAD LISTENER

Tonight, I stood in the same shop doorway past closing time on the corner of Pine and Saint Laurent Boulevard and busked "Starting Over." The song always makes me think of Mark David Chapman, Lennon's murderer, who stood outside the gates of the Dakota waiting for an autograph from his prey. Lennon and Yoko Ono had been working in the studio that fated evening.

"Mr. Lennon," he called softly. Then dropped to his knee and put five shots in Lennon's back with a .38.

There wasn't a soul around, the sidewalks were deserted. But tonight I kept strumming, my back stuck to the brick wall, and in that position I asked for the next winter passerby to be you, Spit. I asked for the impossible, I did, throat raw and eyes glassy, I set my magical thinking to the tune of Lennon's sappy song. In black army boots, guitar strapped to my chest, I performed a modest, hoarse opera and asked for the next face to be yours.

How I wanted you to find me singing that song, how like a child I felt. My back was up against the wall, and in that posture, I recalled the black-and-white shot of Lennon and Ono from *Double Fantasy*. Why that record? Because Transformer reviled it. Because you egged him on when he was at his most humourless. Only you could do that, ridicule him, and come away unscathed. You were the only person able to get away with that. On the back cover, Lennon and Ono are standing against a brick wall facing Central Park across the street: Yoko, the Inscrutable; John, Vulnerable John, looking especially fragile because he's not wearing his glasses. *Double Fantasy* was part of our inheritance, and more than fifteen years ago when I first picked it out of the pile and presented the album to him, Transformer turned it in his hands—dismissing the kissing front outright—to have a look at the back.

"Check it out," he said, without missing a beat, "Easter Island in New York. Overlooking traffic, not the fog. It looks like John's prepared to face the firing squad. Except he can't see who's out there. A safe bet says the enemy are music critics."

Sharp. I'd noticed the vulnerable side of Lennon myself in other photographs—him seeming all face without glasses, appearing alien and shy—and to tell the truth, I didn't like it much. Near-sighted to a detrimental degree, he looked sort of helpless and nude. I concluded in the day that anybody who wears glasses shouldn't ever take them off. Our braggart counsellor from Bethune, Mr. Dawson, had a similar thing happen to him whenever he stopped talking bollocks for a moment to remove his glasses and rub the bridge of his nose. I've always remembered that. How without his glasses he, too, looked over-exposed. Mr. Dawson had that in common with Lennon, the near-sighted eyes of wounded larvae. Ironically, I could say the same about the baby-faced assassin, Mark David Chapman.

Why am I telling you this?

"Don't fuss about the details!" That's what you told me days after we met in the hospital. "No regrets. Please don't remember me like this. Please, no wasting time." Rather, you wanted to hear about my song writing in the last years and about the future you were going to miss. The thing is it's hard to separate music from my feelings about the past. But you knew this would be difficult, didn't you? When I protested and said that I wouldn't know where to begin, you shushed me, waving two fingers.

"You don't have to be a technician about it!"

Fair.

"You'll figure something out."

Spit, you promised me you'd be such a good dead listener that form would hardly matter. You're probably right. I cannot think of a more attentive group of listeners than the dead.

Transformer and I used to talk this way with the lights out, listening to records or radio during the interlude before sleep.

Can I ask you something?

Maybe.

In the upstairs bedroom. That summer we shared everything.

Do you get lonely?

Staying up late until we made no sense, it wasn't really talking then.

What are you talking about, Hombre?

It was thinking aloud.

Nothing.

Just before falling asleep, we'd play at word association.

Rapid.

Lob something.

Eye.

223

While staring up into the darkness.

Movement.

We'd keep at our game until sleep knocked us out. Shoot the shit until we got so tired our voices changed. Then we'd drift off under a constellation hanging from the ceiling. Every night, we left a new arrangement in the sky, some few dead stars too.

Because   Radio   Aliens   Europe
Beggars   Paranoid   Oomph
Quiet   Inheritance   ELO   Borg   Dummos
Patti   Punk   Spit   Incubation   Heads   Morfar   Wells
Vets Wave   Disco   Busk   Muswell   Shrooms
Plagiarism   Harmonica   Leprechauns   Revolver
Dawson   Pusher   Gauguin   Megan   Allamuchy
Pigs   Dope   Faithfull   Plants

See? There you forever rest, perfectly suspended between punk and incubation.

GROWING PAINS

PARTY

We're going out.

"Have fun, boys." Flowers stands at the bottom of the stairs and reaches out to touch us both on the chest as we troop past. *Have fun... not too late... be careful... don't get yourselves killed.* This is the mantra since time zero.

"Don't forget your purses," Candy hollers from the back room where she's camped out with the house Swedes to watch a Victor Borge comedy special on TV. Victor Borge is a Dane, but that's close enough for this clan. Borge is a comedian who plays classical piano. His formal whimsy and gentle personality remind me of Morfar.

"Jealous," Transformer grumbles in response to Candy, and we are out the door and headed to a basement party to see the band called the Slins. The band was profiled by Megan Lynch a week ago in the *Chronicle*. The patchy photograph accompanying the text showed four undernourished rascals in a city playground, hanging from kiddie monkey bars. Juvenile delinquents or hardened criminals of the post-rock underground scene, it was hard to tell.

"That makes us soft as babies," says Transformer as we traverse the bird streets. "Did you know the brothers in the Slins are twins? The younger one is like you, Hombre, only fifteen or something."

"But you said they were twins."

"Doesn't matter." He keeps marching. "Twins come out separately, don't they?" Stops to light a cigarette. I'm struggling to keep up.

"We'd better hurry," says Transformer, rubbing the ciggy on the front of his shirt. "We don't want to be late."

The party is being held about a kilometre beyond the bird streets, in the new development where until a few years ago there was just a bunch of straggly bushes and some woods. We would venture here to have little fires at night. It was like camping. During the daytime, we'd pick through broken glass and firecracker shells and the waterlogged magazines. Mostly we'd sit on burnt logs and read from *Penthouse Forum*. But after the '76 Olympics, the city planners put in a McDonald's across the highway and built the overpass that fed the developers, and the new houses started popping up about a year ago, eliminating our fantasy jungle.

The front door opens to a vacant ground floor. Halfway down the wooden stairs to the basement, Transformer stops ahead of me and ducks under to have a look around. It's cave-dweller dark with shapes along the foundation walls. Hieroglyphics. Sand blasted by music. There's a table for the stereo in the corner but no stage area that I can see, no amplifiers or drum set or anything.

"There's Darren," Transformer whispers.

"Where?"

Against the wall. Sitting with Nick. Darren has a mohawk now, which must mean that he no longer listens to Supertramp. Nick is wearing a threadbare "I Tripped Terry Fox" T-shirt.

"Nice sentiment," Transformer says.

Right.

Transformer steps down into the basement and begins talking up Darren and Nick, and I can't get his attention now for a good while until I go ahead and hit him on the shoulder.

"Do you think Spit's here?"

"I don't know."

"Julie said she'd come early." But I don't see Julie either.

"She did?" Transformer shrugs and then turns back to Darren and Nick, who are manoeuvring, trying to show something. I am not invited to see.

"I guess she wasn't too impressed by our last gig, eh?"

Transformer turns around. "What are you talking about?"

Nothing. Transformer has no sense of humour and no memory; he invited Julie to the party in the first place. Not me. I invited Spit. But I don't think Spit is coming. The music playing astounds me. The sound is crappy. I tap Transformer on the shoulder.

"Who is this?"

Transformer inquires among his new best friends and comes back with the answer. "Ripcordz."

"Who?"

"With a Z."

Good name. Transformer disappears again but returns soon with new information. "They're from NDG or something."

"They must really hate how things are," I say.

"Grow up," Transformer says, "it's punk rock."

I get it.

"Grow up or stay in the vein where you belong."

What is that supposed to mean? Last summer when the Marathon of Hope was coming to Montreal, Flowers took us by bus downtown to welcome Terry Fox to the city. Terry Fox had had a leg amputated to stop the spread of his cancer, but still he pushed ahead, jerky gait on a prosthetic, completing twenty-six miles a day. A day! I kind of wish I had the balls to wear Nick's stupid T-shirt, but I don't. Maybe that's a sign. I wish Spit was here for company, or at least one of the Willeys. But the Willeys don't attend parties. Not when they could be building a nice little fire inside the Pine Beach underpass. We call that structure the underpiss. The passage that runs under the highway and joins the service roads smells deadly. A fire might cure that stink. Neil and Gavin Willey aren't full of outrage. They love fire.

Looking around now, I notice this one kid with an electric guitar in his lap, a small audience formed at his feet. I get up and walk over. It's Chris Burns of the Terminal Sunglasses. How could I miss him? He's scary skinny and has this narrow head that juts from his shoulders like a shark's fin. He's wearing round metal shades even though it's murky dark in the basement. People like me respect Chris Burns even if we don't really know him. I've been thinking about that since we busked. He has an aura despite asking for nothing. Right now, he's playing his guitar unplugged and making this plasticky off-kilter sound and squeezing patterned notes out of his hands, making it look easy. When he strums hard like a machine that's deranged, everybody loves it, especially when he begins singing. His facial expression says it's berserk to be singing anything at all.

The little crowd can't hold back.

Come in! You can leave your mind outside!
You can leave your mind outside!
Come in! You can leave your mind outside!
You can leave your mind outside!

That's really funny when you think about it.

I turn around, and two members of the band are hovering behind the DJ table. In blotchy flesh, the Slins have appeared like a bad Xerox copy of their own poster. Minus the bassist and drummer. Just the brothers are on hand.

News spreads quickly that the band is not going to play the party. It's enough that these two Slins took the bus from downtown to visit a wasteland. They've got this normal kid with them handling sales of their EP, *Suck Yourself.* Price: ten dollars. I can tell that neither of the Slins is that eager to chitchat. Another thing I notice right away is no way these two Slins are twins. There's too big an age difference. Megan's profile was off. Transformer's knowledge of biology is limited. They came out separately all right, something like four years apart.

Meanwhile, the DJ turns up the volume, and a bunch of kids rise to the occasion and begin bashing into the grey metal posts that are everywhere. The cave dwellers come out from the walls and join the fight for dance space. Fifteen or twenty hominids start orbiting their own death wish. In the mix is Megan's friend who I saw at Station 10, the Bowie guy who is flying out of control and crashing into people. Someone like him would have livened things up at our show at the Vets. As a musician, on principle, I don't dance. The DJ is in the same boat, marooned on his side of the stereo system.

"Do you have any Clash?"

DJ squints. "What?"

"The Clash."

The DJ stares at me like I'm moron meat. Like I'm a leper. Should shake a leg, move along. Forgive me for asking.

When I locate Transformer again, he's down with a small posse and sitting cross-legged with his shirt raised and his neck bent forward. As I approach, a bunch of kids get up to leave, shaking their heads and making faces of disbelief. This one girl sticks a finger down her throat. It's not Julie. Or Spit. Meanwhile, Darren and Nick are egging Transformer on.

"Do it, do it, do it."

"What's happening?" I shout at him from the outer ring. Transformer does not hear me or pretends not to—the music is raging, and he's performing. Suddenly he jumps up from sitting and pulls his shirt off his body, and everybody starts clapping. He's performing all right, waving a wand in the air. It's only an incense stick. After sitting back down, he glances in my direction and I'm finally back on his radar.

"Hombre," he calls my name.

What are you doing?

It's him alone in the crowd. Him and him and him and him. Just hearing him say my name aloud for a second makes me feel a bit better about tonight.

"You try." He reaches for me to grab the burning end, the tip glowing in the dark.

"No."

"Just try."

He's got Darren by his side like Darren's his girlfriend tonight. His pals both have burn marks up the arm. They've been busy. Transformer is branded below the ribs. He won't hold eye contact with me, but he beckons. "Come on, try it."

"No."

"Join the tribe," says Darren.

"What?"

"Just do it once," Transformer sweetens the bargain with this once-in-a-lifetime opportunity. "And you're in."

"I said no."

"Why not?" Nick challenges me.

Because zero face.

"Use this instead." Darren flips a bottle cap into the air. I toss it away. Nick blows his bangs from his eyes. "Right."

"He doesn't *feel* like it…" Darren's loving this.

I don't feel like any of this. I take the wooden basement stairs and exit to that familiar refrain.

Come in! You can leave your mind outside!
You can leave your mind outside!

This party's been a blast.

BOYS

When Transformer gets in later that night, he goes straight into the bathroom and doesn't come out for a while. I can hear him running a bath. I listen for when the faucet is creaked off, then for a dull thud as my brother climbs into the tub.

"Can you come for a minute?" *Knew it.* Transformer's come to get me, wrapped in a towel. I follow him back down the hall.

"Lock it," he says, re-immersing himself in the water, wincing. I sit down on the toilet beside the tub while Transformer laments: "Fuck, that hurts, that hurts, fuck."

"Shit, Transformer. What did you do?"

The anarchist in him has outdone himself: burned a couple of spots into his flesh and also carved a zagged "A" on his belly.

"Lots of people do it."

"Like…?"

"Darren."

"You should see a doctor."

"What are you talking about?"

"Doesn't it hurt?"

"It kills!" Transformer bends forward and gently laps water onto his stomach. "Fuck, fuck, fuck a duck," he says while goosebumps break out on his skin. "Give me the towel." He's about to stand from the water when we hear faint knocking at the door.

"Boys?"

Transformer rolls his eyes.

"Boys…" It's Morfar. He keeps a blue plastic jug by the bed. That way he doesn't need to get up in the night to pee. After a third knock, I'm sure it's him.

"Boys? Your grandma needs to use the head."

"Don't open it," Transformer says.

"We have to," I say.

Not according to him. Not without a useless fight. He gestures for me to throw him that towel and then steps out of the tub. I wish he would hurry. Transformer stands there and dabs at his spots while I grip the doorknob.

Outside in the hall, Morfar and Mormor are standing together against the wall, she in a white nightgown, he in an undershirt and shorts, leaving us just a bit of room to step out. Both have this crazy wild electrocuted hair, as if for old people like them getting up in the middle of the night is terrifying. After we pass, they go inside together and I overhear Morfar saying, "That's better."

Afterwards, about five minutes later, Morfar stops by our room and opens the door a crack to whisper, "Thank you, boys. It was an emergency."

"Did you hear that?" I say to Transformer, who already is standing before the mirror dressed in pajama bottoms, admiring his work.

"It doesn't hurt that much anymore," Transformer says, turning from side to side to view his arms and stomach.

His burns and blisters. His cut belly. The new look fits him satisfactorily. But it turns my stomach. Him and everything. The image of Mormor and Morfar waiting in the hallway has shaken me more than anything. Morfar's scary legs: skinny tubes jutting out beneath his shorts. Skin saggy at the point of his elbows. A prominent potbelly. Meanwhile, even if Mormor has kept the skeleton away by eating plate upon plate of kaka, something has been going on since the end of summer. She's on the fragile side. Her presence is wavering. It's no longer the time for taking sun, is it? A chill has set in.

Since the party, I've been in my own head. Candy knocks.

"Can I talk to you?"

Who asks permission? Nobody. Nobody except some-body who wants to tell you news you don't want to hear in the first place.

Candy kicks a shoe under the bed and sits down tight beside me, as if there's only one small park bench to share in this room. Lays her hands in her lap.

"What are you working on?"

"My songs."

"'Fuck Creation II'?"

"Yeah."

"Well, good. You're doing great, Hombre."

But what about it? She draws a deep breath. "Can I ask you something... Have you noticed anything different about Transformer?"

"No."

"You sure?" She lets it hang, her question, but I'm no snitch. "He wants to drop out of school."

"I know." I didn't, but it figures. "So?"

"Come on, Hombre."

"What?"

"Mom's really worried about him."

"She is?"

"Yes. She is."

"Why?"

"You tell me. I mean, you're the only one who spends time with him. Does he seem different to you?"

He is different.

"You two have something special." She bites her lip. "A special bond. Sometimes Mom and I wonder if you share brain cells or something."

"Scientifically speaking, we might."

Candy and Flowers do lots and lots of we-thinking around the kitchen table, usually at night after Candy returns home from her shift at the Vets. If any two people in the family share the same point of view, it's them.

"Plus…" For a second, Candy is distracted. She pauses mid-sentence to admire Bjorno's racket grip. It's been a while since he put a spell on us. "You have all your music and the band."

"It's just me and him."

"I know. But it's more than that, right?"

In a way it is, and in a way it's not. In a way, the band hardly exists. The new demo means something. It's supposed to put us on the map, help with getting gigs. But I'm beginning to think there is no map in the first place and, meanwhile, we're just hanging out in our room, jamming and listening to records when we're not smoking on the roof. Everything's a long shot.

"Anyway," she frowns. In no rush to leave. Something's up.

"Where is he?"

"With Mom," she answers matter-of-factly.

"At her work?"

"No," Candy says. "Not this afternoon." And leaves it at that for an elastic second or two, before adding, "They went to see the doctor."

"What do you mean?"

"Don't worry. Everything will be all right. Mom's going to ask him to move into the basement for a while."

"What's going on?"

"I can't tell you." She stands. "Keep at it," she says to shut me up. *Keep at it. Carry on.* It's military language. It's code for building your life, for progress. What about Transformer? Did Flowers and Candy discover his new hobby? I haven't told a soul. Transformer and I haven't spoken about the party or his disfigurements since the night of the long knives.

CROSS-EYED

When Transformer returns, he runs the stairs, flings open the door, grabs his Stratocaster, and starts playing it loud. In sympathetic fashion, I reach for my Ibanez and join that noise. After something like twenty minutes of blind jamming, Transformer stops and tells me what he has.

He has a sadness meter.

"That's what the doctor called it." Transformer shoots off a riff and sustains the sound by pinning the strings against the neck of his guitar with real venom.

"You saw a doctor?" Candy wasn't lying; well, I knew she wasn't, but still.

"Where have *you* been?"

Nowhere. Just here. I've been waiting for somebody to tell me what's going on. Transformer gestures for me to get in line and copy what he's playing, and out of nowhere we start rolling off some twelve-bar blues. Blues are about as avant-garde as peanut butter. We are crap at this. Transformer spoofs a spaced-out solo while, underneath him, I lay down the bars one after another like I'm building with Lego. Bar chords kill my hand, a pinpoint cramp between thumb and index finger is at the root of the blues for someone like me. Spit says it's because of my positioning. After a few rounds, Transformer wants to talk some more.

"Dr. Wells explained that it's like a light meter on a camera but the opposite. My thingamajig looks right into people for the dark spots."

"How?"

"Like a regular X-ray. That's why sometimes I prefer not to go to school. High school is a minefield."

"Will you have to take pills or something?"

"Nah."

"What's his name again?"

"Who?"

"Your doctor."

"He's not *my* doctor. Dr. Wells. But I guess he's this big downtown shrink. It doesn't matter."

Transformer shrugs. What doesn't matter? He can see dark spots? Just after he made Dr. Wells sound like a superstar MD with a bunch of platinum diplomas hanging on his office wall, Transformer is laissez-faire about the whole deal.

"We're on opposite ends of the spectrum," Transformer says. "I grow feelings. Dr. Wells shrinks them."

Is that what a shrink means? I ponder this while Transformer hops onto the desk and shuts the window. A jumbo jet releases thunder overhead.

"He shrinks them because he's a shrink. Get it?"

Yeah.

"I have tons of feelings."

He's all over the place. Not everything is real. The band is hardly real. His sadness meter doesn't sound real. But lots of things can *turn* real, which is a thing Neil Young sings about. *When it's hard to make arrangements with yourself.*

242

When you're old enough but young enough to sell. What the hell does it mean though? It could be worth Transformer asking Dr. Wells.

"Did you show him your scars?"

"These?" Transformer lifts his shirt. "I'm proud of these little babies. Yeah, he's seen it all."

"What did he say?"

"Not much."

"He didn't tell you to stop?"

"My body."

Your body needs help.

"Was Flowers in the room?"

It needs protection.

"Not all of the time."

"Well, he might have spoken to her after he saw you."

"What's wrong with you, Hombre?" Somebody please tell me.

"You don't get it."

No.

"Insight is the trick with these kinds of things, which for your information is sort of like looking inside yourself."

"Dr. Wells said that?"

I'm asking too many questions. All goes quiet on the Transformer front. I get the feeling this balloon of silence is damaging and might last a while, so out of the blue, as an offering to him, I say, "Spit has shrooms." But this new information doesn't register because Transformer's sadness meter is attuned to more interesting signals than his little brother talking about Spit's secret stash. I bet he's looking into himself and has a lot on his mind. I bet insight is a trick you can do without using a mirror. In a minute or two, Transformer has risen into a sitting position and begins to explain where he got his thing from in the first place.

"I probably got it from Flowers, the original sad eyed lady of the lowlands. She cries a lot. Did you know that?" I did not know that. It had not crossed my mind. "Flowers sees Dr. Wells too. She's one of his." I did not know that either. "I'm pretty sure I got this gizmo from her. But don't worry about it, you're safe."

"I'm not worried." I'm not. Because I don't understand. "What about Candy?"

"Candy—no way."

Why not? Why not me or Candy? Transformer sounds like an old hand at this already. He eases over onto his side to face the wall. "Good night," he mumbles into the pillow.

"Good night."

ENCORE

After about fifteen minutes, Transformer says, "Hombre, are you still awake?"

"Yeah."

How does he expect me to sleep now, after introducing Dr. Wells, after telling me about the original sad-eyed lady of the lowlands, after calling high school a minefield? And after Candy's visit.

"Do you still want to talk?" It's not me with a light meter. Transformer's a shadow when he sits up. "When I watch people like Flowers, I feel sad. Sad as hell sometimes."

"Why?"

"I don't know. That's what I need to get used to. Some people are worse than others. People on the bus. Old ladies when I'm collecting. Sometimes my meter goes off the charts. The worst is Mormor."

"Mormor?"

"Yeah. She sends a strong signal. She listens every hour to the weather forecast, but she never goes outside anymore. Plus, she's superstitious. Did you notice she kicks the air, twice, every time anybody leaves the house?"

She's always done that. In the morning when I leave for the bus, she waits at the window. She watches me go until

I'm out of sight. I'm used to it.

"It's gotten worse," Transformer says. "Something's going on."

"Like what?"

"I don't know. But I'm picking it up."

"Maybe it's just because she's old and beautiful."

"What?"

Nothing. I don't really understand what we're talking about. *Maybe because you love her* is what I really wanted to say. *She's old, beautiful, and you love her*. That's why she makes him sad. Probably.

"With this thing, I can't go out much. I'll move into the basement to be safe. Although the trick is to learn when to turn it off. And only use it wisely. When it's appropriate."

"When is that?"

Transformer doesn't answer.

I hazard a guess. "Like keep it for a funeral?"

"What are you talking about?"

No clue.

Would that be overkill?

NIGHTWATCH

I was swimming against a tide. Just exhausting. Same as last time. I tried forcing my way up from the sandy bottom but kept getting pushed under.

"Congratulations on having a scary dream." Transformer is awake before me. He's still here, not yet cloistered away in the basement where it's safe.

"It was a nightmare," I say.

"Then congratulations on your nightmare. What was it about?"

It was about him. And his thingamajig. "I don't know."

"Forget about it then."

"It felt so real. I was terrified." In the dream, Transformer was standing over me, looming beside the bed.

"Why?"

"I don't know. I couldn't move."

"Hombre." Transformer gets up on his elbow. "You were dreaming."

"But I still woke up feeling scared."

"Of what?"

Of you. Of him and him and him.

"Can I ask you a question?"

"Is it a trick question?"

"Did you watch me last night with your thingamajig?"

"You're out of it, Hombre."

It goes without saying.

"Do you know what they say about dying in your dreams?" No. "Well, they say you can't die in your dreams. So don't worry, Hombre. It's impossible. And if you dream that you're dead in a dream, then it's over and you are dead."

Who told him? Probably Dr. Wells.

"It's simple. If you died in your dream, then you'd be dead."

I'll miss him when he moves into the basement.

FAITHFULL

All we do is talk. I'm supposed to be having my private lesson. I'm at her house in the birds. She's got some new posters. REM, Siouxsie and the Banshees, and Marianne Faithfull have squeezed in next to Robert Plant. There's hope yet he'll get the message and come down off the cross.

"What's Transformer doing today?"

"He's gone with my mom to see somebody."

"Who?"

"I can't talk about it."

"Mysterious." She slaps her knees and starts humming the lyrics to the song playing. I sit at her side and stare at my own feet.

"Who is this?"

Spit points to the blue and black poster of Marianne Faithfull. She's tired, dangling a cigarette and shielding her eyes, from drug fatigue probably. The end of her cigarette is coloured this fake glowing red. It sets a mood. Spit grips my hand and knocks it on her leg to the beat. "*Could have come through... Anytime. Cold lonely... Puritan.*" It's a catchy song though Faithfull sounds fed up, spiteful of the melody. Still, I'm hooked. Beside me, Spit drops into a kind of trance while she sings along. "*What are you fighting for?*" And I get the sense the words mean a lot more to Spit than they could to anybody else, almost as if Marianne Faithfull had Spit in mind when she wrote these fighting lyrics.

"*Lose your father… your mother, your children*." Spit's performing it, working on stage presence maybe? I'm leaning like a bag of sand by her side.

After the fade, Spit doesn't miss a beat. "Where did you get all those stories about your grandfather?"

"Search me."

"He worked on a ship, didn't he?"

"Yeah."

"Didn't he run away once?"

"Yeah. More than once." I feel proud saying so.

"What about your father? You don't talk about him."

"I told you. He died at Expo."

"No, you didn't."

I think I did.

Spit says, "It doesn't matter."

It does, but it doesn't.

"Hey, what's Transformer doing again?"

"I just said, he's gone to see somebody."

"That sounds mysterious."

I'm not supposed to tell anybody, but why not. "He's seeing a doctor."

"He is?"

"I just said."

"A doctor doctor? I saw a shrink once."

"You did?"

"When I stopped eating."

"You stopped eating?"

"For a while. Not anymore. What's he going for? His vow?"

"Probably, yeah. And other things. I don't know."

"If you ask me, he talks a lot."

"I guess everything has to do with the way he's feeling. He goes to sleep early. He runs out of things to do, I guess, and then he just goes to sleep."

"Like at what time?"

"Eight. Sometimes seven."

"Jesus." She squeezes my hand.

"When I stopped eating, it was because I wanted my father here. But that wasn't going to happen. Mom hates him. Sorry. I guess it's not fair talking about my father this way."

"Which way?"

"Like he's alive."

But he is.

"I got really into music instead and started eating again."

It doesn't add up.

"When my brother gave me all this stuff—guitars, drums, and a bass, it saved my life."

I squeeze her hand.

"It's fucked up," she says.

"Yeah."

"But it's not so bad."

"Should we do something?" I mean, like pick up our guitars and play?

"I don't feel like it," she says.

Me neither. This is better. Doing nothing.

SCREWDRIVER

I lie on my bed and stare at the empty wall space Neil Young used to occupy. I can almost still see him up there: his big guitar and a metal harmonica brace and for him a real microphone to sing into because he's playing a gig to thousands of people who came just for him.

"Be quiet," Transformer says.

I place a pillow over my eyes.

"I can hear you, even when you're doing that."

He must mean even when I'm doing nothing, when I'm just thinking about what it's like to be someone like Neil Young.

"You make a lot of noise."

"Sorry."

"Yeah well. I'm taking this apart." Transformer is sitting at the desk with his back to me, turning a screwdriver.

"What is it?"

"This thing." One of the ionizers from downstairs, like the one Morfar used to sell door to door until his legs gave out. Transformer's detaching a wire. But why?

"Don't ask," he says, anticipating my question.

"I can leave," I say.

"Don't bother. I'm almost done. Anyway, I'll be moving

into the basement soon," Transformer says, "where I can get peace and quiet."

"I'm sorry."

"Don't be."

I'm not used to this.

DEAD LISTENER

This just in! I have news for you. Tonight, I went off list. Normally I never pause between songs. I plough through my set. Each song falls out and follows in order. But tonight, it was different. I took a detour. Usually that's a fatal error, an invitation to the blues. But this song fell out of me. It *played* me. And then there was this girl of about thirteen, standing a little further down the street, tapping her foot, just hanging out; you know, my biggest fan, born three minutes ago. Dressed in her school uniform, carrying a backpack, she was not in any rush to get home. That was the first unusual thing I noticed: someone of her generation stopping to listen and sticking around. Who was this person? Afterwards, she dug inside her backpack and approached with some change in her hand, only to be taken by surprise when she noticed there was no collection hat or cup for tips. She just let go of loose change by my feet, like she was spreading fertilizer.

"You didn't have to," I said. "Thanks."

"Sure." She answered. And walked. But only seconds later, she returned. "Hey, who sings that song?"

"What song?"

"The one you just played," she said. "I really like it."

"It's old."

"Yeah, I know." She didn't skip a beat. "I haven't heard it in a long time. My mom, she used to like it."

Who *was* this kid? Confused, for a moment she made me think of you, Spit, as she stood there, serene, like she had all the time in the world. Geologic. Eventually she said, "I want to play guitar one day."

"How old are you?"

"Fourteen."

"That's a perfect age to start."

"Maybe…" Then she left, not so sure playing an instrument was in the cards, and straightaway it came to me. I sing that song. Me. Hombre.

Hombre wrote that song.

There's no way this kid knew what she was talking about. *She hadn't heard it in a long time.* What did that mean? Still, she liked what she heard. I'll take the credit for that. Do you know what song, Spit? I'll sing it now. "*I never meant what I said. Can't you tell when I'm playing dead?*" Once upon a time, it was about us. But now? What's its meaning? Who would know better than the kid, the stranger, my lone fan, if it means something entirely different today than it once did to me or to you? She came walking down the street and innocently crashed right into that song, and the music must have served as a bridge for her. That's what I think. Sorry about all the pseudo-philosophizing, the bullshit, but I'm doing my best to wrap my brain around this, which brings me around to song writing.

And to the bridge.

The bridge is pure mysticism. It promises hallelujah: an eventual celebratory return to the sunshine of the chorus. The minor chord twist before the break of dawn. Often, it's damn flakey. It will make you cringe: Do we *have* to go there? Who put this fucking thing at the end of the song? Must we cross over it? Can it take our weight? All kidding aside, without a doubt, the bridge presents a Cartesian moment. There is no turning around once standing on that metaphorical bridge. Either you transcend—and continue across to clouds of poly-phonic sweet harmony on the far side—or the abyss beckons. Where you have your hopes dashed on the rocks.

Why am I telling you this? I'm still warming up. We'll cross that bridge soon.

A REAL CHANCE

PONCHO

Transformer and Spit go in ahead while I wait outside on the curb clutching my purse as traffic squeezes by brightly on Sainte-Catherine Street. The air smells like perfume. The sidewalk swims with people dressed for a Friday night. Soon the doorman from Station 10 steps out for a smoke. Showtime.

This time it's a different guy, just this tall kid in a grey wool poncho.

"Do you *like*?"

The doorman positions himself for a duel like a gunfighter, his hands hovering at his side before he fast draws and, "Bang."

I tell him straight, "My mother makes those."

"Really?" The gunfighter takes a tight drag. Squints. Repeats, "*Really*?"

"Yeah. You're wearing a poncho, right?"

"Compadre, you are correct."

Hombre… Compadre… sounds friendly. It works and rhymes without reason, and I'm on a mission to get into the club underage. For the record, Flowers is a weaver. She has a loom. It's in the TV room. I used to sit on the bench behind the moving parts and pretend I was driving a tractor while watching *Hogan's Heroes*. It was like having farm machinery inside the house. Flowers made a poncho and two or three shag rugs. But after six months, the rugs began to smell strongly of puke. Our dog Jolly was dying. I consider telling the doorman this episode of our family history but think better of it. Poncho's been sizing me up.

"Hey, listen, Spit told me about you and the band. She's a friend. A friend of friends, which means you're a friend too."

Really?

"If you can keep your head down, I mean a low profile, I can use the company." Poncho nods towards the entrance. "Stick around near the back and help me do the door."

My lucky break.

Inside, Poncho leans against the wood bar. Station 10 is tight and narrow just like Spit described it to us on the bus ride downtown a few weeks ago. It's packed wall to wall. When the crowd shifts just a bit, I get a good view of Three O'Clock Train because the stage is backlit.

"So what do you play?" he asks.

"Guitar."

"Good answer. Who else is in the band?"

"My brother."

Poncho nods like he knew it all along. "Isn't she in the band too?" He glances towards Spit, who is standing with Transformer against the wall a bit further in.

"She plays on our demo."

"That's all right."

"She was the engineer too."

"An engineer, eh?"

"Her older brother Paul runs a real studio."

"Connections," Poncho says. "Like I said: a friend of a

friend is a friend. You need them. Connections, I mean." He peers over the mass of heads. "Have you seen the Train live?"

I shake my head. Negative. Eliminate the cretins I saw at the Moustache and my brush with the Slins, and I haven't seen anybody live.

"Then this is your lucky night. I do the door whenever the Train has a show. Do you have a manager?"

"Kind of."

"Managers are dicks."

Everybody says that, including this Poncho here. Managers are fabled fools. As of a week ago, ours is Duncan Ridgeway. Transformer is bewitched by this Duncan guy, one of his classmates from New School. "He's got business sense" is the line Transformer fed Spit and me after shaking on the deal without telling us. "Obviously, yeah," Spit deadpanned. "Obviously, business sense is esoteric to you, isn't it? Something edging on mystical to all the young dudes who attend art school?" "You'll see," Transformer countered. "I bet," Spit snorted like she does. And I didn't say a thing. Then for his first move, Duncan prints business cards. But Duncan gets it wrong. He prints two hundred cards without listing a phone number or contact address. For his second move, he encloses said business card plus demo and sends our press package out to *The Gazette* and the *Chronicle*.

"You don't need a manager until the band has a record to push," Poncho continues, pushing his variation on the theme. "Maybe in a few years. But you brought the demo?"

Affirmative. I feel inside my purse. I don't leave home without it. Neither does Transformer. We bring the demo wherever we go.

"Can I see it?"

I show him.

"TDK." He turns it in his hands. "Four Song Dummos." Hands it back to me. "You're serious." Taps a cigarette on the bar top and signals two beers. "You're going to want to talk to Mondou." He scans the crowd. "Mondou books the bands. He's in the basement. I'll call down."

Poncho grabs the telephone from behind the bar and presses a finger to his ear. I've lost sight of the others. I bet Spit found a friend. For someone who tells a lot of dead-baby jokes, she makes friends easily. Then there's Transformer. Where is he? Making no friends at all. I wonder what signals he's picking up in here? It's dark enough. He has X-ray vision, doesn't he? The beers arrive. Poncho slides a bottle downstream.

"Drink up," he says. "Without delay."

I tip the bottle and stare down the neck into the bubbly insides.

"Go on," Poncho encourages me. "How did you hear about the show tonight?"

"*The Gazette.*"

The Train ends one of their songs to applause and whistling. "House favourites," Poncho says. "They're brothers too."

I can already see that.

"Mack is the song writer and lead singer. His brother Stu holds down lead guitar. Together they make sweet harmony." Poncho doesn't remark on the other two members. The bass player is standard. He's doing a job, bricklaying; he and the drummer are supporting cast. "What do you think of 'Dark Country'? Lepage coined the phrase for their

266

sound. He comes in sometimes." Poncho takes a quick look around. "Not tonight."

Dark Country. I can see that. Country and rock, with some punk bleeding through. It's not a bad thing. Right about now, Mack begins telling the tale of a fake honeymoon. He stands front and centre, gripping his guitar. Mack's eyes are shining as he muscles into the no-good heart of this motel ballad. His brother Stu sure looks messed up—all wire and sinew—a body beleaguered by proud trouble. When Stu sings harmony, his gentle smile surprises the shit out of me. Stu has the type of role in the band I'd want for myself if we get famous: that of the sideman who is free to wander to the outskirts of town at the edge of the stage and get into all manner of mischief but who always makes it back into the thick of home after, to sing harmony during the chorus. Plus, Stu has a set of loud groupies. "Stu!" his groupies go. Every time, Stu lets go this goofy underdog smile.

Poncho knocks me on the shoulder. "Check out the talent scouts."

"What?"

Nods towards the two men sitting at the bar. "A&R."

I pull a long blank face.

"Artistes & Repertoire."

"Really?"

"PolyGram."

That quiets me. The stuff's tangible. Make it or break it right here. And here comes Transformer without Spit, swimming through the crowd to join us at the back of the club.

"This is my brother," I say, feeling grown-up making introductions. "And this is Poncho."

They shake.

"Julie's here," Transformer whispers sidelong in my ear, "and she brought her people, too, for once." A good-sized group, I can see. When I look over, Spit's loving their company. Her smile is alive. Her eyes too.

Poncho tips his beer towards Transformer. "So you're in the band? And you two are brothers, right?"

"We must be," Transformer says.

"That's cool. Lots of bands use two brothers." Poncho points towards the stage, and I don't know if it's all the noise in here or something else, but that expression sounds weird: lots of bands use two brothers. *Use them*? Like in an experiment? Against their will?

"How old did you say you were?"

Transformer stares off into nowhere. He's not going to say. I won't either, in case Poncho remembers his duties as the doorman tonight.

I tap Transformer on the shoulder. "See those guys at the bar?"

Transformer turns to look.

"Thieves from some big label."

"In here?"

"A&R."

"Tell me about…"

"Ask Poncho."

Poncho delivers on cue. "Apes and Rejects."

"WHERE ARE THEY FROM?" Transformer booms.

"Take it easy," Poncho says.

This is as close to getting signed as we've ever been. Just the fact that A&R men have shown up in Station 10—likely to have a look around for the second coming of April Wine—means revolution is in the air. Soon there'll be new blood for FM radio. Transformer has no fear. He cups his hands into a blow horn:

"KGB or EMI or RCA or CIA or BMG or FBI?"

The inside joke we have is about a cold war between Montreal and Toronto and a record business run by foreign agents and promo squares from the Don Valley. The reps travel in pairs and prefer to slip into a club like Station 10 incognito during the live set and skedaddle without leaving a trace, although rumours always go around after: *Some reps were in tonight! They caught half of your first set! It looked like they were really into it!* The labels are in cahoots with FM radio, and the big boys keep a shortlist of who gets airplay stored on microfilm back at headquarters. In total, that list may comprise of ten supergroups from the sixties and seventies and five new-wave bands from the eighties, so a total of fifteen that the superpowers are willing to gamble on. This we know. This we hate. This has always been. Oh yeah, with a flick of the switch, these A&R types can instigate a coup, and before you know it, you could be the next Billy "brown-nosing" Joel, a real big shot.

Transformer has their number.

And he isn't shy.

"KGB or EMI or RCA or CIA or BMG or FBI?"

SIMULACRUM

Poncho leads us to the back of the club, through a metal security door and down the greasy steps into the basement.

"His office is just around the corner."

Mondou lives down here in a cramped storage space, from where you can *hear* the band playing upstairs but, sound-wise, we're underwater. Poncho rounds a pile of crates and boxes, and we come upon a red door. Before knocking, Poncho points to the peephole.

"Smile," he says. "You're on Candid Camera."

Transformer walks right up and puts his eye to the hole.

"Security." Transformer whistles. "The Great Rock 'n' Roll Swindle."

"Whatever you say," says Poncho.

"Punk rock," says Transformer.

While we are made to wait, big brother performs. "Bob Dylan got a parking ticket. Chuck Berry ugly... Jagger white... Dury Cockney Fraud!"

"Cool it," Poncho says, stretching his hands deep in his pockets.

"Bowie blond runt. Rod Stewart got—"

The door buzzes, unclenching its teeth. Poncho pushes it open and in we go, and immediately you can tell this Mondou guy behind the desk loves the colour red. The brick walls. The fuzzy carpet. The filing cabinet. Even the desk, which has this gigantic layer of glass lying on its top. Everything is red, even the plastic blow dryer lying side down like a revolver in its own surface reflection inches from Mondou's right hand. The only exception: a solid black rotary telephone awaiting news from the outside world.

"These are the guys I called down about," Poncho says.

Mondou raises his eyes for a moment, then lowers them again and draws a figure on the piece of paper before him.

"Sit down."

There's nowhere to sit but the sofa, which is occupied by Mondou's muscle, busy blowing on his fingernails like they might be wet.

We remain standing. Mondou's hair is greased and swept across his scalp in trenches. It looks like some animal landed on the top of his head, slipped, but then still managed to hang on.

"What can I do for you?"

"They have a demo," Poncho says.

Mondou raises his eyes and then pulls a desk drawer open only to close it again. He's misplaced something. His glasses? He's got a pair wedged on top of his forehead. Things aren't moving fast. "Do you have a card?"

I'm not going to answer that.

"Do either of you talk?"

Transformer finds his voice. "Is it your birthday?"

"This one has a mouth."

"What's with all the red?" Transformer says.

Mondou flashes a grin. "Better red than dead." Sofa-man pounds his knee as Mondou gestures to Poncho. "Put it on.

Let's hear this."

Poncho slaps the cassette into the tape deck, cues the first song. Meanwhile, there is the muffled impression of Three O'Clock Train rolling overhead. The first twenty seconds of the demo play. Mondou scratches his ear.

"Where's the rest of the band?" He begins pencil-drumming the telephone's shell. "Don't tell me you're a dippy folk group duo?"

"They're not." Poncho comes to our defence. In my blind spot, Transformer smoulders. He'll blame the folk influence on my criminal past, the many hours listening to Simon & Garfunkel, sucky tender moments crying with Flowers while listening to Joni Mitchell.

"Sounds like it." Sofa-man spreads his legs wide and flicks at his balls. Spit should be down here. She'd say something witty about now, like: "Big man bored for castanets?"

"What's the name of your band?" asks Mondou.

"Because."

"Because, eh? And you don't have a card? All right, Because, are you ready for the big time?"

Station 10 is not big time. It's a dump. The bottom rung. But playing here would be better than busking. Busking is futile. Busking is drowning on big mouthfuls of nobody-cares-about-you while coughing up oceans of oblivion. The experience is draining. People get in your face or else they walk right past you without noticing. I haven't developed any presence. None whatsoever.

"That's why we're here," Transformer answers, sounding like a true vet. "For the big time."

"There's no money in it," Mondou grumbles.

"We don't care."

"You drive a hard bargain," Mondou says. "Probably live with your Mommy."

To which Transformer inexplicably responds, "We're running out of time." I check sideways—are we? Transformer is looking straight ahead. I'm not in the picture.

"What are you talking about?" Mondou scoffs. "You're just getting started."

"I didn't mean that," Transformer says.

"Kid is bold," Sofa-man says.

Mondou turns to me. "What's your name?"

I mumble the code name Compadre since Poncho is standing right next to me. Mondou shakes with disbelief. "Who the hell are these kids?"

"Stubborn motherfuckers," says Sofa-man.

Poncho laughs nervously. "They're nice kids. Brothers."

"No joke," says Mondou.

"Sorry." I fumble an apology.

"Are you pulling my leg?"

Transformer blurts, "We can bring people."

"Sure you can," says Mondou.

"What kind of people?" Sofa-man says.

"Julie has friends," I offer up.

Transformer glares at me.

"Who's Julie?" Sofa-man smiles.

"Just a friend."

"A girlfriend?"

"Girlfriend, eh," Mondou says. "Mommy allows that?"

"We don't live at home," Transformer says.

"Then where?"

"Somewhere."

"*Somewhere.*"

"Outside," I say.

"Outside," Sofa-man repeats after me and flicks the eight ball.

"You guys are a gas," says Mondou. "What other *people* can you bring in?"

"We can get a crowd," Transformer pipes up. "We have a manager who can get the word out."

Mondou's turn to laugh. "You boys on snow?" He leans forward and pinches a nostril and snorts a patch of air from the glass top. "Are you? Because you're not acting very bright."

"I know."

"*He says*, I know! Did you hear him?" Mondou engages Sofa-man. "He said: I know."

"I know," says Sofa-man.

Mondou pours on the gravel. "Listen, kids, I can pay you in snow. Now, I know what you're thinking: *He just said there's no money in it.*"

"We don't need to get paid."

I am talking for some reason.

"They don't need to *get paid.*" Sofa-man making a mockery out of the obvious. "*Get paid.*"

"I heard him," Mondou says.

The demo ends with our song "From This Room," and Mondou comes around. "I liked that last one. You might have something. I'm thinking…" he says while Sofa-man taps his gonads in disbelief. "Listen, boys. We have an afternoon slot next month. Friday and Saturday afternoon, opening for the Darned."

We take it and run.

OOMPH

"You need more oomph," Spit says. "What if you join my band and I join yours?"

"What's the difference?" Transformer says.

"Instrumentals," I say.

"My band needs exposure," Spit carries on, "and you guys will need a little more oomph or else you'll get blown away."

Mondou and Sofa-man pop into mind. She's right about the Station 10 gig. The Darned will most likely hit the stage hard and in seconds annihilate any folk memory of Because. But does she really have a band? I'm on bass in her band. We've never practised. And I don't play bass.

"I have a better idea," Transformer says. "Why don't we form the same band?"

Spit says: "That's what I meant."

Not sure that she did.

"I like this idea. Playing live is murder. The audience is the enemy. With three of us up there, we can blast them with a wall of sound."

"Keep the Huns at the gate." Spit's got the idea.

"Spit, you play bass," Transformer says, getting into it, "and we can get Neil or Gavin to pound on the drums."

"The twins?" Spits says.

I'm as surprised as her. And taken off guard.

"Yeah," Transformer says. "Probably Gavin. Gavin is more punk."

Raised eyebrows from Spit, as she must be thinking the same thing I'm thinking: how can he tell?

"Call Gavin now," Transformer says, demanding action. "Get him on the horn."

I get on my way to Flowers' bedroom to use the telephone. Neil answers after the first ring, like he's been waiting for this call, and I tell him the news.

"Sure," Neil says. "I'll tell Gavin."

Before hanging up, I roll the loaded question down the line: "Hey, which one of you is more punk? Transformer says it's Gavin." Silence ticks. "Forget it. Just come over. Bring your drums. We'll be practising downstairs because Spit's in the band too. On bass. We just found that out today."

Sounds of silence.

"We're in her band and she's in our band."

He'll figure it out.

"Playing live is murder."

Breathing.

"We'll need everybody's oomph."

Click.

Vertigo. Putting the phone down, I feel drunk and giddy with changes that happen without warning and all at once.

"I talked to Neil," I say, relaying the information. "I told him everything. They're both coming over."

"Both?"

"I think so."

"Okay," Transformer says, "that'll work."

Pondering the new line-up, he steps on the chair and onto the desk and squeezes through the window. Spit follows him outside onto the roof, carrying her weighs-a-ton electric bass leather-strapped to her chest. By the time I get out there, Transformer is crouching close to the edge and Spit is up against the siding of the house, posed like a punk guerrilla, finger-tapping her four-string bazooka. I find shade and, from where I'm sitting, become aware of the groundlings below taking autumn sun. The usual crew minus Mormor are assembled in lawn chairs. Spit hisses to get my attention. When I turn, she pretend-pouts and points her bazooka into the sky. She's just playing around. For the record, Spit will give us a whole lotta presence. More than Transformer and I mustered at the Vets anyway.

"This will be an experiment," Transformer says.

Yeah, a live experiment.

"What songs should we practise?"

"We only need five," Spit says.

"Five or six," he says.

"Shouldn't we tell Mondou?" I ask.

"What are you talking about?"

"Nothing."

But I mean telling Mondou that we're adding bass, drums, and oomph.

"What about a practice gig first?" Spit says. "Something small to get us ready."

"Practice gig?" scoffs a crouching Transformer.

"I'm serious," Spit says. "What do you think, Hombre?"

We need to jam, to practise, and we need to become a band. We don't become a new band by immaculate conception. That's what I think. But I'm not one of the visionaries.

"You can enter the Battle of the Bands at John Abbott," one of the groundlings hollers from below. It's Candy. She's been eavesdropping.

"What did you say?" Spit asks.

"The Battle of the Bands at John Abbott. They're always looking for acts. It's a bit late, but I can get you on the bill."

"We have a manager," Transformer says, reaching into the neverland depths of his jeans pocket.

"Voila." He flips our business card into the air.

Because
Manager Duncan Ridgeway
Entertainment and Live Groups
MUSIC FOR ALL OCCASIONS

The card floats and lands in the eavestrough.

"Since when?" Candy says.

"Time flies in this business," Transformer says. "We had to act fast with the new demo."

Duncan Ridgeway, Dorval's Malcolm McLaren. The fabled one of no phone number. Him of no contact address. Just as well Transformer is tossing cards into the wind.

"Your sister's only trying to help," Flowers says.

"Oh hello, Ms. Lindstrom," Spit says.

"Hello there, Spit," Flowers replies, shading her eyes.

"Hello there, Fart," Transformer says.

"Hey da," Morfar says.

"Where's Mormor?" I ask.

"Inside," Flowers responds, staring into the sky.

"Is it too cold for her?"

"She's tired today. She'll come out tomorrow."

Since when is somebody too tired to sit in a lawn chair? Anyway, Spit is playing her bazooka. Even when that thing is unplugged, the thick strings make a racket.

"Spit is in our band now," I say.

"That's nice news." Upturned face.

"We're getting a drummer too."

"You'll be a real band soon," Candy says.

"You're a real genius." Transformer draws a line over his throat.

"What will you call yourselves?"

I give Spit and Transformer a questioning look. They are the visionaries. A new name didn't come up. Why not? Transformer kicks the rooftop and sends a shower of pebbles down.

"Slonotars?" Spit says.

"That's better than Because," Candy says. "I kind of like both."

"Heaven almighty," Transformer says.

"What say da?" Morfar says.

"Watch your language," Flowers says.

Spit begins whispering to explain herself. "Since you two play really slow… slow on guitar. I thought Slonotars was a good name. Get it?" We both nod. Spit expands: "We'll perform like we're very tired and play everything loud and slowly like we don't care."

"I like it," Transformer says. "Slonotars."

"Great," Spit says.

I have no say.

"The name of this band is Slonotars." Transformer launches into it.

"Why?"

"Because we play slow guitar."

"But you suck!" Spit does her best smart-ass heckler.

"Get off the stage!"

"Shut up!"

"Get off!"

"I fuckin' told you to shut up!"

"What's going on?" Flowers asks.

Nothing.

"We're just fooling around, Ms. Lindstrom," Spit says.

"What the difference?" Transformer says.

I know what he means.

SLONOTARS

While we've been fooling around, the Willeys have gotten down to business. They are on the move. I've been watching their progress from the roof: the twins emerging from their back door, the first carrying the bass drum over his head, the second holding snare and high hat as well as a rectangular black case under his arm. Now they are right up to the fence.

Hands full, they dump the drums over the fence first and climb into our backyard.

"Hi, boys," says Morfar.

The twins continue out of sight, on their way to the back door.

"They must be in the house," I say.

"Let them set up," Transformer says. He's not moving, showing who's boss.

"I'll go," I say.

"I think you better," Spit says.

By the time I get down to the living room, they've assembled the drums. It's a five-piece silver set, though the toms are blackened. Encrusted with what looks like fire damage.

"Gavin?"

"Oi. That's me," says he, adjusting the high hat.

He *is* more punk.

"What happened to your toms?"

"He always lights them on fire. For the spectacle," Neil says from behind his keyboard.

"How many shows have you done?"

"Zero."

But he always lights them on fire. With gasoline jelly, I bet. Therefore their melted status. The twins no doubt will add more oomph. Be their own kind of live show. But the keyboard is a surprise. Transformer won't be happy. Sure enough, here comes the boss now.

"You can't play that."

Neil drops his head. Dabbles keys, spins the volume dial, and the keyboard emits a huge empty sound.

"Leave him alone," Spit says. "Let's see what it sounds like first."

Her comment sets the stage for some awkward murmuring while Spit and Transformer and I set up our amps and plug in and arrange ourselves in a nucleus of proximity like a real band.

"What are we called?" Gavin says.

"Slonotars," Spit says.

"The name of this band is…" Transformer says.

"Slo-no-tars." I do my part but I'm still feeling out the new name. As are the twins by staring at the ground, from what I can tell. After a good ten seconds of this ground gazing, Neil surprises the shit out of me with a suggestion:

"Why not call ourselves Sugar Mountain?"

"Sugar Mountain," Gavin repeats.

Sugar Mountain. For a band name, it's not bad, but it makes a fuzzy first impression like the song itself. The country fair, the barkers and balloons, the girl beneath the stairs.

"That's not bad," Spit says.

"Yeah. But we already have the new name," Transformer says.

"Nothing lasts forever," I say, pushing my luck.

"Nope," Spit says. "Nothing."

"Forever fucking young," Transformer says.

"Fucking young forever," Spit says.

Neil blinks.

"Is this how we're going to talk?" Gavin says.

"What do you mean?" I ask.

"In the band," Gavin says.

"He means when we're onstage," Neil says. "Do you want us to talk like this?"

"Are you stupid?" Transformer says.

Intense gazing between the twins through their channel.

"Let's try something," Spit says.

"Do you know any of our old songs?" I say.

By old songs, I mean the early stuff from two months ago.

"Songs by Because?" Neil asks.

"The back catalogue," Transformer says.

"Remember you saw them at the Vets," Spit says. "Did you buy the first tape?"

"What's it selling for?" asks Gavin.

"God in Fuck's Creation!" Transformer says.

"Hit it!" Spit says. No count in: Gavin slaps the snare. Spit starts rolling on bass. Transformer and I crunch way down on guitar. Meanwhile, Neil does a wavy dance behind the keys. It sounds just perfect. I sing into the light bulb. My adrenaline running wild. Nobody knows how to end the song. We keep it going until Candy enters the room waving her arms.

"I'll let you know by tomorrow if you're on the bill," Candy says. The twins give her a double take. *Like where did she come from?* "You might have to do covers though."

"Covers are for…" Same old thing.

"You're just rude," Candy says.

"Thanks for the advice," Spit says.

"We need to practise," I mumble.

"Hello, everybody." Flowers appears inside with Morfar by her side. "Who is staying for dinner? Everyone is welcome."

Kiss of death.

CHANGES

All the young dudes have dinner at our house. Afterwards, Gavin and Neil and Spit go home to get set for dress rehearsal tomorrow.

In bed, my mind is going through these changes: having the Willeys and Spit as new members of the band and then our new name, plus the practice gig at Battle of the Bands, before a real gig at Station 10. We only started digging three months ago, and now we have two demos and a manager. Copyright is still witchcraft. One afternoon, Candy came to ask me if I've noticed anything different about Transformer, and the same day Transformer came home proud of his thingamajig. He read my diary. It all started when Spit flew out of the bird streets to mentor us. I think about her all the time.

"Be quiet, Hombre," Transformer says. "I can hear you."

"I wasn't doing anything."

"Yeah, well, I can hear you thinking."

That makes two of us.

Transformer has invited Darren and Nick to be judges. Duncan comes to devise promo. Julie shows up without people. Candy and Uncle Per fill out the room.

"I'll print new cards," Duncan says. "With the new name."

"Address and telephone are the same," Transformer says.

"I've got it this time," Duncan says.

"That's using your business sense," Spit says.

Duncan flips his empty hands in the air as if to say *what's the big deal.* I'm following the banter while tuning my guitar.

"When do we start?' Gavin asks. In jean shorts and wearing no shirt, he is definitely the punk one. Neil is outfitted like the Elephant Man, his head stuffed in a paper bag with holes cut out for eyes. Spit is wearing her Ramones T-shirt. Bjorno strutting his stuff in a headband.

"We look not half bad," Transformer says. "What are you going to wear, Hombre?"

"Nothing."

"The emperor's clothes, eh?" Darren says.

"Leave him alone," Spit says.

"Standing up for your boyfriend."

"Yes, I am," she says.

"Good for you," Julie says.

My face tightens.

"What's going on?" Neil says.

"Our dress rehearsal," Gavin says.

"Are you taking any requests?" Darren says.

Transformer steps on the distortion pedal, letting loose some Bad Company.

"Do that!" Darren or Nick.

"You'll never win Battle of the Bands," Candy says. "Unless you play covers."

"U2!" Nick hollers.

"You can win studio time," Candy says.

"It's worth it!" Julie says.

"We've got the Fostex," Transformer says. "Who needs a studio?"

"It's debatable," Spit says. "Let's get started. Hombre, come stand by me."

"The lady's man!" Darren says.

"Loverboy!" Nick shouts.

"LOV-ER-BOY!" Darren and Nick. "LOV-ER-BOY!"

Neil watches the ground beneath his feet. Things are getting out of hand, and we haven't played a note yet.

"Hit it!" Spit says.

"Not yet," Transformer says.

"Chicken!" Darren or Nick. "Turn Hombre Loose!"

"Put something nice on, Hombre!" Must be Duncan.

"Leave him alone." It's Julie.

"What's going on?" It's Gavin.

"Why are you talking suddenly?" Transformer asks.

"He does that," Neil says.

"I'm leaving," Uncle Per says.

"Don't leave yet," I say.

"Me too," Candy says.

"Good riddance," Transformer says.

"Oh boy," Spit says, and she starts thundering on the bass. That gets everybody going. The band is ablaze in seconds, and four songs deep into our set, here comes Mormor walking down the stairs.

We stop hammering, astounded that someone of her age is among us. Spit bends down to unplug a patch cord to let the beauty pass. As Mormor makes for the end of the couch, Duncan and Darren and Nick make for the door.

"What's wrong, Mormor?" I ask.

"Leave her alone," Transformer says.

"She's amazing," Spit says.

"She can hear you," Transformer says.

"Are you going somewhere?" I ask.

No answer. In the interval as we await her next move, we go suddenly motionless, holding our collective breath like swimmers at the bottom of a swimming pool keeping still so as not to disturb the clarity of the moment. But it doesn't last. In my peripheral vision, I catch the shape of a wind-milling Pete Townsend. Spit's eyes are begging Transformer to stop. The place is about to blow when Morfar and Flowers appear in the doorway.

"We're taking Mormor to the doctor," Flowers says.

POPPIES

In grade ten English, we've started reading *Canadian Poets of the Great War*. Service. Roberts. Trotter. McCrae.

In Flanders fields the poppies blow, between the crosses, row on row.

Everybody quotes those specific lines, but what gets me is this.

We are dead. Short days ago, we lived.

Transformer moved into the basement.

How can that be?

BOMB

Flowers talks in circles. "There's nothing anybody can do… I understand it's a shock for you… We can set up a bed in the living room… Your sister has experience. It's too late for the hospital. There's nothing anybody can do."

What does she mean it's too late for the hospital? If it's too late for the hospital, for doctors and nurses, what are we going to do for her at home?

"The doctor will make home visits. When it's time. We don't know for how long."

"So she's a ticking time bomb?" Transformer says.

"Be quiet," says Candy. "Are you stupid?"

"Please don't talk that way." Flowers reaches across the surface of the table to grab all our wrists at once, but it's not possible. Instead, she squeezes her hand into a fist.

Opposite me, on the kitchen wall, are many versions of the Tomten. The hard men of Swedish folklore, as we've come to know them. Out prowling the straw-filled barnyards. Flowers is decorating for Christmas. She begins earlier every year. This is her favourite season. The Lindgren posters are the first to come out of the Christmas box, before the wood reindeer and red candelabras. By Christmas Eve, this place is Sweden.

"What about Morfar?" I ask.

"He's handling it well. At least it's not a surprise."

It isn't a surprise?

Candy speaks with authority, from experience. "He's upset, which is expected. And very emotional."

"Can't she go into the hospital?" I ask.

"No, honey. She'll stay with us. You don't have to worry. We're all going to do this together."

But do what together?

"She's accepted it," Candy says. "I've seen it happen at my work. For now, she's accepted it. That could change, though. There are phases."

"She's brave." There. I've said it.

"Yes, she is," Candy says. "She'll be ready. She is brave."

"Let's get on with it then," Transformer says sourly.

Flowers leaves the table to run hot water in the sink and, after testing it, she places her hands under, purses her lips, and makes a hissing sound.

"What is *wrong* with you?" Candy drills Transformer. "I'm glad you moved to the basement."

"Ready to die?" he shoots back. "How would you know? How do you know who's ready?"

"It's an expression, idiot."

"That's the problem with you," Transformer replies.

"Here we go," Candy says.

"It's just another—" He stops right there, mid-speech, with Flowers having moved from the sink to behind his chair. Running her hands through his hair. Like he's the one who suffers the most. Like he's the one who needs her attention.

"Just shut up," I speak. "I guess you think you know everything because…" I begin to expand to the surprise of everybody. "I guess because of your stupid sadness meter…" However, I never finish my sentence because right at this moment Morfar and Mormor appear in the doorway.

The two of them holding hands kind of blows my mind.

LAWYERS

After knocking, my voice searches for the right register. "Can I come down?"

"Just you."

"Sorry about what I said upstairs."

"Don't be."

Transformer is seated on a chair that he's set up beside the furnace. He stares into it through a tiny window like it's a real fire. It stinks like oil down here. He has a lamp, a bed, a table for a desk. He didn't bring any posters down to decorate. No Bjorn Borg or Patti Smith. He left them upstairs with me. Now he lives here like a tenant, with the washer and dryer for company. And in the corner, the sump pump. The sump pump smells gross when mice drown in it. I never liked coming down here before. Not to hide or to spy. The basement is no playground. Transformer's quarters are limited by three half walls and a crouch space that stretches into the dark. He has no window. There is no taking sun.

"How long do you think you'll stay down here?"

"Until I work things out."

How long will that be? If he really wants to move back upstairs, according to Flowers, this could take a few weeks with the help of Dr. Wells. Because of him, Flowers wants me to see Dr. Wells too. She's booked an appointment. Next thing, I'll be living down here in the basement trying to fix my own thingamajig. I might talk to Mr. Dawson instead. He has his own diploma.

"There goes any practice gig," Transformer says, ploughing ahead with his own thoughts.

"Why?"

"Because soon Mormor will be logging time in the living room. No more rehearsal space until: *ka-boom!*"

"Was that a joke?"

"Everything's a joke these days."

"It doesn't have to be."

"Grow up."

"Mormor might get better. They don't know everything."

"Weren't you listening?"

"What about Station 10?" I ask. "That's real and not a joke."

"Sail on, silver girl. In one hundred and fifty years from now, will anybody care?" I don't know, and I don't follow.

Transformer is intently watching the orange glow through the little window. It must be a billion degrees inside the furnace.

"Is this place even safe?" I ask. "How can you stand the smell?"

"Oh, come on. It's not so bad. When we die…" Transformer is focused on watching the dancing shadows. "…are we really going to care about having played Station 10 or about who gets all the credit for 'Fuck Creation'?"

It's unlikely.

"Know what I'm talking about?"

Not really.

He's beginning to sound like an old man. "Nothing means anything. The only choice is between revolution or royalties." It might be the oil fumes, but *Revolution or Royalties* strikes me as a catchy title for an album. "Lawyers and the law only exist so that you can steal things legally." *Revolution or Royalties* might sell more units than *Into the Ground*, Transformer's initial idea, which to me sounds like the kind of album capable of burying itself. On the front cover, I see the band dressed like guerrillas in a desert holding machine guns and Spit sprawled Sphinx-like with some fake pyramids of gold coinage piled in the dizzy distance. "And that's where copyright comes in. Copyright is theft. It's stealing property from the collective unconscious. You wrote all that stuff about finding songs in the sands of time and fossils…"

Everybody sounds like somebody else these days. That's part of the problem. Even I do, in my diary.

"Hombre, you can't own the music of the spheres. Can you?" Probably not. "But trust some lawyer to come up with a price tag."

"Fucking lawyers," I say, because he wanted to hear it.

DOOZY

I'm drowning in rhyming couplets. Poetry about sacrifice and butchery—the whole sorry song read aloud by lethargic fifteen-year-olds seated in cemetery rows. Slaughter in child rhyme. To be excused from class, I raise my hand and go see the man.

First thing after knocking, I say, "Do I need an appointment?"

"Never in your short life," Dawson says, shuffling his pile of desk papers. "Sit or stand. That's one doozy of a decision."

I stand. Twice a month I come here, but this time I feel different. I hang out by the wall for an eternity, studying Dawson's diploma—the imprimatur, the flat poppy—and then the picture of Lennon's crushed spectacles, the memory flash of his blood-speckled ovals lying on the pavement outside the Dakota. The photograph was on the front page of newspapers. FM radio was all over it too. Last December, Transformer came here feeling lost on the morning of Lennon's murder, and Dawson gave him this pretentious speech about the stuff we are made of and the insubstantial pageant and yakked forever about John being a dreamer first and last, as if that meant anything. Transformer was hurt at the time and furious about it.

"You understand Latin?" Dawson interrupts my reverie. "Cum Laude. Different from cum-loaded. It means I graduated with distinction, above the average."

Dawson took his teaching degree at Oxford. He can sound intelligent even when he talks bollocks. Not knowing or understanding what Dawson is talking about is fine, just fine for everybody. Including me. Most of the time.

"What's on your mind?"

There is a long list of things beginning with Transformer's basement residence and his sadness meter. Spit. Spit on bass and Spit wanting me to do shrooms. Station 10. Meeting Mondou and Sofa-man and rehearsing for our opening gig. The Darned. Banshees. Tomten. Revolution. Taking care of Mormor when the hospital can't do it. Turning punk before it's too late. Oil, gas, and dismemberment. The Battle of the Bands. Poppies that blow.

"Hey, seriously." Mr. Dawson stands. "I can see you're feeling blue, but everything's going to be okay." He motions to the chair. "At times like these, it helps when we become a little philosophical." Here we go: the speech, shall he begin filibustering his brains apart about the flesh as he did with Transformer? But wait: Dawson pokes his nose out into the hall, before turning the lock and gingerly stepping to his place behind the desk.

"Scotch?" He pulls the bottle from the drawer. "How many fingers?" Pours. "A tumbler for two." Laughs and mumbles. "Doris Day?"

I've heard of Doris Day, and I've heard of this, the bantering, the offhand way the chosen are initiated into Dawson's tribe. If I'm honest, I was feeling left out.

"You know what a tumbler is?"

It is a squat thing.

"Czech crystal."

Glassware scratched crisscross in design like a snowflake.

"Take."

I receive it with both hands and bring the tumbler tight to my chest.

"Hot toddy it's not."

No sir.

"Listen, my mistake. This isn't a good idea. Not right now. I want you to come back after school. Can you do that? Return after last class?"

"My last hour is gym."

"Perfect, young man. We can talk this out later. Do you need a note to get back into class?"

Saying what?

Already don't I wish it was morning again and I was back in
Flanders Fields and I hadn't raised my hand. I could be on
the bus right now going home.

"You're a real Scotch drinker, aren't you?"

First manly mouthful tastes of dung.

"Take another pour."

Of smoked horseshit.

"Listen up. This life is of the utmost. For you and for
your brother, who through different channels I have come to
understand is under considerable pressure. For the likes of
the Because brothers and the brethren, I ponder these matters of the utmost."

He raises his glass. What channels? The amber is harsh,
a blitzkrieg on my afternoon intestines, and after swallowing
I turn and spit tummy nectar into the wastepaper basket.

"I'm feeling a bit sick," I say.

"That too shall pass," Dawson says, and then doesn't he
give me the full speech. "Individuality is major. In high school,
it is of the essence. It sparks rebellion and delinquency and
all of it. A person like you, in the larvae stage of life, should
want to become like no one else. That's your birthright. All life
really amounts to is becoming yourself. I'm not talking about

solipsism, which to the brethren is a form of blind masturbation. You understand that, don't you?"

Cum laude. Come Lord. Cum-loaded. He said he said he said he said. People like Mr. Dawson talk and talk until you can't hear yourself think. Until you sink headfirst. Whatever cum laude really means, Dawson graduated full of shit.

"This is about you, young man, becoming you. That might sound weird to you at this present moment, but trust me that later it will not."

"I guess."

"Believe me, it will not." Dawson pours me more drink and grabs a handful of mints from the bowl with his other hand. "Go ahead," he motions. "Take." He packs some greens into his mouth and begins rubbing his eyes after flipping his specs onto his forehead. "I've had a day." He blinks and rubs his eyes with rounded fists, grinding until whatever sight he had must be squashed. But he keeps going. "Impersonate every other pipsqueak on the planet, right, or live your own life. That's what I'm talking about. You've read *Catcher*, right?"

People of Mr. Dawson's generation recommend it and like it more than kids my age, which used to surprise me. The book is part of the curriculum. Transformer hated it. An example of child labour, he called it, because the author makes Holden do all the work.

"With the kid?"

"Holden."

"Right you are." Mr. Dawson is beaming. "I suppose you'd be the expert."

Not really.

"You know what I think? Holden is paralyzed. Figuratively,

300

of course. The future terrifies him. Same for his insane brother. Maybe that's what Transformer feels? Have you talked to him?"

Do I talk to my own brother? I stand, ready to leave but woozy.

"Hey, I'm sorry to hear you're feeling blue. It's going around this time of year. What do they have you reading in there today?"

"*Poets of the Great War.*"

Dawson pinches his nose. "Square as grandpa's glasses, stinky as grandma leaking old age gases. Do your grandparents still live with you?"

What kind of a question is… the amber, the mints, the war poetry. I let him have it: "Rhyming is the last refuge of the scoundrel."

"Sharp, young man." Dawson's voice is strained, a note of dissonance bleeds through. What else did Transformer reveal to him, through what channels?

Straight off the bus from school, in the side door, and down the stairs into the basement. Lost for momentum and out of breath, I gotta tell Transformer about Dawson.

"Drop your purse and sit," Transformer says.

Case an open casket on the floor beside his bed, guitar balanced on his chest, Transformer has waited for my return.

"I've got something to show you."

I offload my purse, take a seat.

"Are you ready?"

Transformer begins to sing:

I'm an introspective—dope —
—I'd hang myself—
—If I had enough rope—

That's him all right. He's not paralyzed. I love the beginning of the song so much, for the moment I forget about my time in Flanders Fields.

"Sing that part again," I say. But Transformer takes no notice of me, and after cycling through the verse and chorus, he arrives at the bridge:

When I wake up—
—I'm all aglow—
Because of all the things—
—I don't know.

"Don't stop, Transformer."

If I had my guitar down here, I'd be working against the grain, fingerpicking and turning out something sweet and mesmerizing to accompany him.

"That's all I have," Transformer says.

"It's new territory."

"Maybe."

Not maybe. The melody is sly. The lyrics are strange and funny. The words are him. His personality. There's more to come, I can tell, but not today. Transformer's not in the mood. Show and tell is over. Visiting hours too. The dope's just lying there, blanket pulled across his shoulder and turned to face the wall, wrapped in his own juices like a mummy.

"You okay?"

"I don't feel well. That's all."

"Because of Mormor being sick?"

"I don't know."

"Is it your thing?" His thingamajig.

"I'm going to sleep."

"Now?"

"What's the difference?"

It's four-thirty in the afternoon, that's the difference.

"Hey, Transformer." I try to lift him. "Should we get your song ready for Station 10?" Add distortion for the intro and we won't sound so hippy dippy. Mondou will applaud it.

"If you want," Transformer mumbles.

"The lyrics are good."

"Thanks."

"When did you write them?"

"This morning."

He sounds irritated. At some point during the day, Flowers and Candy disturbed him by carrying his dresser down from upstairs. It's sitting by the wall close to the washer and dryer. The basement is no cure for anything. Gavin next door moved into his basement to get away from Neil. A lot of teenagers move into the basement, usually with a set of body-building weights and a bed but not much else. It's like moving into a halfway house within your own home. I wouldn't be surprised if Transformer dreamed nightly of tunnelling out through the foundation.

"Can I tell you something?"

"What?"

"I had a weird day at school," I say.

"Huh…" A few inarticulate sounds of the beast.

"I left English and went to see Mr. Dawson."

"Why did you do that?"

"To get out of class—"

"—just to talk to Dawson?" Away to the wall.

"Yeah."

Transformer rolls over. "Did he offer you Scotch?"

"No." I don't want to get into it with Transformer anymore.

"He will." Head on the pillow and eyes at dead rest. "Did he call you a person in the larvae stage?"

None of it made any sense. Or made me feel any better.

"Or mention blind masturbation?"

"What?"

"Blind masturbation. Have you talked to Darren?"

"Why?"

What about Darren?

"Never mind." Eye roll. "Don't worry about it then. Forget it. He's a hypocrite."

"I know."

Transformer turns away to face the wall again. "Goodnight. Turn off the light at the top of the stairs."

Good night, good night, sweet brother. Goodnight. Before supper time!

"Hey, Transformer."

It's not five o'clock.

"What now?"

Nothing.

DEAD LISTENER

Relying on memory is like spinning a record counter-clock-wise to capture the hidden truth. In your honour, I did an experiment. I backward-listened to *Led Zeppelin IV*. Message received. SERVE ME! The garbled voice of Master Satan. FOLLOW IN THE DARK. Deep throat! THERE'S NO ESCAPE. Beelzebub! COME TO ME. Lucifer! The fact is a Christian anti-rock crusader named Jem Something discovered this voodoo and now Christian Jem is taking Zep to the Supreme Court and suing for damages, alleging the band sought to program the subconscious and corrupt the youth with subliminal devil worship.

Well. Look out, Socrates.

Here's the thing, though, Spit. Has Jem or any of these Supreme Court wigs ever taken a moment to listen to the real lyrics on some of these records? Never mind playing them backwards. Play them forward at 33 1/3 rpm. I'm thinking that most people miss the point, and that when it comes to lyrics, we're lost in our own heads. When the radio plays your song, the needle plunks down into the old grey matter and a hymn emanates from within your own being. I believe that's called high fidelity. It's the kind of thing happening right now while I'm lying down in bed looking at the ceiling and at the same time opening a channel just by thinking of you.

We're at the bridge, Spit. We are close, and there is no other way forward. I wouldn't be surprised if you saw it on the road ahead and hid your face in your hands. *It wrecks everything!* I don't like it either, but facts are facts. I abandoned you. I left you for dead, in your side-rail adjustable bed. I turned my back. I boiled the kettle to make the tea and dragged a chair bedside, and with you holding on, drifting in and out of it, we talked a long while. You were on the way out of this world. It wasn't right. It isn't fair. The truth is from the day we met—from that afternoon we came upon you in the store playing the guitar above your head—from the time you arrived at our house to mentor and torment us, you've been many miles ahead of the story. Leagues more mature. Miles and leagues ahead of me.

And now? Too far away. Antarctica.

After drinking tea, you fell asleep, and for a good while I sat in the chair and watched over you as promised, with the understanding that I would wait for the cavalry to arrive. Your family was en route. Your mother and your brother, Paul. I observed your chest rise and fall, I wiped cold sweat from your forehead, I did my best to stay in one piece. We had an agreement, but that evening I abandoned you. Conehead, you caught pneumonia. You had a fever and chills. UFO-grade lymph nodes. Your breathing was rough. You lay covered up to your neck in a robin-egg blue blanket. And while you slept, tucked into your death sled, I snuck away. I got to my feet, remembering that eight days earlier, following our crazy reckless muse, I had spirited you out of the hospital wearing a toque and winter coat. We had gone by taxi again to the mountain. Hopping inside the cab, I caught the driver evaluating your condition in the rear-view mirror. He dropped the window to throw his butt onto the street. *Where to?* We pointed to the cross on the mountain. At Beaver Lake, I asked the driver to park. It was reckless, possibly criminal, but we were breathless and armed with a plan for that single moment. It wasn't the first time that I had sprung you from the hospital, but it would be the last.

It was snowing atop Mont Royal. The outdoor speakers played our song. "Starting Over" crackled from on high. That sappy song again. On the crest of the tobogganing hill, I sat down behind you on the sled and pushed off, my arms wrapped around you tight, tears streaming down your face and my face, and you turned around whilst we were in motion, and we kissed.

And down we went.

Do you remember? At the bottom of the hill, you raised your arms in mock celebration of our timed bobsled run, then brought them down by your side. I held you close. But within seconds you started trembling. Shaking from cold.

"Now, take me back. I'm ready."

I left you at the hospital's front entrance. You warned me that if I went upstairs, the charge nurse might recognize me and I'd lose everything.

"They might arrest you."

I still lost everything.

BREAKING UP

ROLLING

Spit pinches the end.

"Do you approve of my rolling?"

"Yeah."

"But?"

Nothing. After baking under the sun while watching the Battle of the Bands, everything is beginning to feel a bit theoretical, that's all.

"I know you, Hombre," she declares, exhaling a thin cloud, "I know you too well for you to fool me," which is a comfort of some kind since there's no hiding anything from Spit standing here outside the cinema anyway.

"Should we go in?"

She flicks the lighter and, in a poof, the afternoon is consumed in a conflagration. We had met up earlier on campus at John Abbott College to watch the enlisted musicians inflict terminal damage. Transformer was missing in action by the time Spit arrived, but he and I had come over together riding our bikes from Dorval, all the way out to Sainte Anne's along Lakeshore Road.

"The synths are here!" Transformer hollers, standing high on the pedals, when from a distance the first strains of that synthetic whirr and burr seep into the atmosphere.

"Very chintzy." I echo his feelings toward synthesizer music. The Battle of the Bands is a joke, but at least we are getting out of the house. Getting closer, we can make out the stagehands setting up for sound check. We dismount and begin walking our bikes at a safe forty feet from the stage, when Triple Threat's lead singer starts letting off plosives at the live mike.

"Cheese puffs!"

Clouds of people wearing cardigans and drinking from stubbies come and go and blow across the campus lawn. John Abbott College is a place Transformer might attend for two years after high school. If he does, he will have something to say about the dress code. Cardigans are new this fall; they rolled in with new wave. From the looks of things, the button-up sweater is making headway among all the young college dudes. Transformer is having none of it. He's still right keen on black jeans and cut-offs. The cardigan look is bogus.

"Cheese puffs!" Triple Threat's singer peers out from under an impressive fountain of purple hair, his eye-lined face drilled in nonchalance. Transformer and I find a spot to park our bikes near Britain Hall. Placed at the top of a small hill, the red brick building is four storeys and holds court like a dour old man made of terracotta over the main campus gardens and lawns. In behind Britain Hall, there are these massive greenhouses for the students in the agriculture program. There are other buildings, too, some flat-roofed, some with raised cupolas. Past Lakeshore Road is the lake itself, the same body of water that extends to the end of our street. Lake Saint-Louis, if you want to be technical about it. Lake Saint-Pooey, if you want to be real.

"Cheese puffs!" Still more plosives as a gust off the lake breaches the singer's pirate blouse, making it billow madly like a sail.

"For an encore," Transformer says. "I hope that guy ends up in the lake." We find a spot on the grass and sit among the gathering crowd. There might be two hundred people. I'm about to turn to Transformer and tell him I've noticed that a lot of the new bands from the UK sound haunted, and that there might be some connection between cardigans and synth music, when Triple Threat opens their set with a Hendrix cover. Go figure. Transformer right away starts scratching at his ankle with a penknife.

"So how are you getting on with Dawson?"

"Fine, I guess."

After balancing the point on his knee, he lets go of his hands so the knife drops sideways into the grass. Does it again and again with me watching him.

"Did he have you back in for hot toddy?"

"No."

Sets up the knife. "Honest?"

I'm splitting my attention between Transformer and the band onstage and not answering on time.

"That's good."

Cheese Puffs introduces the members of the band. I cannot make out their names. I guess you need to practise doing introductions like everything else, even with a microphone.

"Have you talked to Darren yet?"

"No."

"He's coming with Nick."

The band lifts off again. Bass and drums are a rumble. Electric piano adroitly plinking. The guitarist drops to his knees to inspect a sea of effects pedals. Something is amiss. He futzes around with multiple settings while the sound cuts in and out. Cheese Puffs is ticked. Meanwhile, the piano player doubling on synth holds her ground as stiff as a courtroom stenographer typing out the seven-note solo. Transformer has had his fill. Darren and Nick show up soon enough. So off he goes with them, expecting to be joined by the Willey twins. He's forming his own tribe. I'm not in it. Left alone, I feel the sun working my skin until it finds a way inside my eyeballs. Unsung Zeroes are about to sully the stage when Spit appears to my left and takes a seat on the grass beside me.

She gestures to the stage. "Close encounters of the synth kind?"

"Yeah."

"Has it been scary?"

"Kind of."

"We could have played this thing!"

"I know, eh."

"Slonotars! The name of this band is… we would have won everything."

"What do you win?"

"Studio time."

A real paradox that, studio time. A realm of infinite highs and disappointments. Expensive heaven, so everybody says.

"How's your grandmother?"

"We don't know yet."

"You're a real family."

"I guess."

"It's good, how your family is taking care of her."

"She's probably accepted it."

"What?"

"Nothing."

"Hey, where's your brother?"

"Exodus," say I.

"Movement of the people?"

"Yeah."

"Wannabees." She says it matter-of-factly and nudges me in the ribs. "Come on, let's go." Joint revealed in the palm of her hand. "Come on!"

After moving my bike to a location closer to the road, we hop on the 211 and pretty soon things get hilarious. En route downtown, we stick out our heads as far out the side window as we can and begin commenting on the weak lawn sprinklers and random tricycles knocked over in a few of the deserted driveways. "That's so hilarious!" Someone is pinning underwear on a clothesline. "That's so hilarious!" People are waiting at a bus stop on the opposite side of the street. "That's so hilarious!"

In a giddy mood, I forget all about him. Next thing, here we are, outside the doors to Cinema V, waiting for my first viewing of the mythic Zeppelin film, *The Song Remains the Same.*

SHROOMS

"Take it." She turns the joint over to me and, under close supervision, I inhale and exhale, rapidly, inhale, exhale, before attempting to return it, as though getting high with her is a relay race.

"Hold on," she says. "I have a surprise for you." A horny lump of nausea forms in the pit of my stomach. She proffers her hand. "Take some. Just a bit."

I pinch a morsel.

"You're going to love it," she says, and swipes the joint from my other hand. She takes a tight haul and is squinting as she crushes the end under her heel. That was a brilliant move. Next, we are bonding against the brick wall, her tongue making things complicated for at least thirty seconds until she withdraws and takes my hand and leads me into the main lobby of the cinema.

"Permission to be beamed aboard," Spit says to the usher, handing the red-clad youth our tickets.

"How long does it usually take?" say I.

"What do you mean?" says the usher.

"Hurry," Spit says.

Inside the theatre, the big screen sparkles like the surface of the moon. Spit puts her feet up on the seat ahead and slouches down low, slapping her abdomen to muzak.

"You know you're not fat."

"Um, I *don't* know that."

"You should throw those pictures away." The ones she keeps under her bed, I mean. Her press kit of cruel fascination.

"Pay attention," she says. "The movie's starting."

The panicked dove is let loose into the brown dawn, and the opening credits tumble over a New York City skyline.

At this point, Spit whispers into my ear something about Egyptians. "Each member of the band has a pictograph, taken from a book of runes."

"Ruins?"

"That's what I said." Resting her chin on her knees, she's packed in tight, fetal in anticipation.

"Do you feel anything yet?"

"Yeah. Nausea."

"Hang on." She grips my hand. Here we go. My first time. *The Song Remains the Same.* A telephone call confirms the concert date at Madison Square Garden, and the band's burly manager immediately dispatches a messenger on bicycle to inform the lads. Cut to Robert Plant and family picnicking by the edge of a stream.

"Watch… they're in Wales—Maureen!" Spit screeches as Plant's diaphanous wife floats onscreen in whispery white cotton.

"Ugh." Spit's mood changes.

"What's wrong?"

"Nothing. Just I don't like children," Spit says as the wee Plants, a boy and a girl, go bathing au naturel.

Cut away to John Bonham riding a tractor until the screen melts, to John Paul Jones reading "Jack and the Beanstalk" to his daughters.

"Fee-fi-fo-fum," I snigger. "Do you smell the bum of an Englishman?" And burst out laughing.

"Get ready!" Spit slaps my wrist.

"Ready," I repeat as the camera goes rogue and wanders waywardly, mimicking a stalker until it finds Jimmy Page sitting by a pond on the grounds of an eighteenth-century manor in Plumpton.

Turning to face the camera, Page's eyes glow demon-red.

"Yikes!"

Someone taps me on the shoulder from behind. "Would you shut up?"

Da-na-na-na-na-nana, da-na-na-nana, nana, da-na-na-nana-na. Ba-da-da-da-na-na-nana.

"Holy flares!" Let us sing of Les Paul Page. Him sporting the psychedelic ensemble comprised of tassels and trousers emblazoned with poppies and planets.

"He's a magus!"

"Astrology!" someone yelps.

Spit's whispering tongue turns like an eel in my ear.

"Ouch."

"Did that hurt?"

"Not really."

Da-na-na-na-na-nana, da-na-na-nana, nana, da-na-na-nana-na. Ba-da-da-da-na-na-nana!

"The fearful symmetry!" the same kid yelps from a seat way back.

Symmetry, for sure—the kid's spot on. Jimmy's noodling triggers vertigo: racing down the scale, back up and around, skipping over the fretboard, down then up the neck, down, through and around. This riff, slap my knee, is an ode to Escher on electric guitar!

Spit scowling: "What pressure?"

"Never mind," I say.

"Then be quiet," she says.

Cut to John Paul Jones, the pale-faced pope of the electric bass. See Bonzo banging his drums like a kid at his own birthday party waiting for some flamin' cake.

Cut away to lead poser. Half man, half beasty. Like a centaur. He makes me squirm! Spit is lip-syncing now. Eating him up. Until—cut! And we go in for a close-up of Jimmy Page picking the intro to "Since I've Been Loving You."

"This is my favourite song," I announce to Spit.

"Since when?" Spit says.

"Since I've been practising. I can play it from beginning to end."

"Cannot."

She's right. Cannot even close.

Plant slips into his horsy phraseology and iterations of *seven-to-eh-leven-to-eh-leven-to-eh-leven*. His nonsense lightens the mood.

"He can sing and shear sheep all night," Spit triumphantly informs me.

"Naturally," I deadpan as the camera pans the crowd inside MSG. Thousands are hand-waving in unison. Like they're washing a giant window.

"I've never noticed how cute you are before," Spit says and pulls my face sideways and tries to kiss it.

"You kissed me face."

"Arrest my!"

Cut to shots of entranced NYPD. It's exhausting. How the lads can go on and on. So many of the songs remain the same fifteen minutes in. I steal a sideways peek and, dear Spit, she's right there, and it's been how long since we've been friends?

Ten years? Feels like longer. Feels like forever. She kisses me on the ear as JP sits down behind the electric organ.

"Thanks for the present," I say.

"What present?"

"Your kiss."

"Oh that."

The camera pans the New York City skyline.

Plant adlibs, "Does anybody remember laughter?"

"It was nothing," Spit says.

Bonzo rides a motorcycle. Bonzo works a jackhammer. Bonzo slings a sledgehammer. He's a one-man wrecking crew.

"Bonzo's all right," I say.

"Yeah."

"It's sad what happened to him," she says.

"I know."

The guy behind taps me on the shoulder. "Story time's over, lover boy."

Cut away to Bonzo drinking ale with his mates at the local. To the racetrack where Bonzo applies a pod-like helmet as his handlers belt him into a race car. While the men in overalls push the racing car onto the paved track, I feel something foreign in my pants. The car takes off. Pounds down the racecourse. Fire squirts from its arse. A parachute pops out. Heartbreaker.

"Don't look at me," Spit says.

"I'm not," I say.

"Yes, you are."

"I'm just breathing," I say.

Newspaper print spins in the whirlwind of a documentary centrifuge.

"This must be a true part," someone in the cinema wise-cracks.

The bass line walks. Guitar joins, in rockabilly-blues mode. Full-bodied, proud, no jerking around. *Boogey mama all night long!*

STUNTS

The world wants in. Not five minutes after my return home. And I've arrived home without leaving the cinema. Time it is to gingerly unzip my jeans. Holy crap. Nothing is recognizable.

Outside the door, Candy's in a panic.

"I was looking for you everywhere. Where were you?"

I was at Madison Square Garden.

"Come on!" She slaps the outside of the door. "Open up, open up!" She sounds so desperate to divulge before she explodes, so I open the door.

"Shit, Hombre." She holds the sides of my face in her palms as though making sure it really is me. "Something happened."

"What?"

Her breathing is off.

"It's really bad."

Transformer.

"He's in the hospital."

"Why?"

She relays the bare bones of the incident: he was on the roof of a building at the college, doing stunts with his pals, using bicycles they'd hoisted up the wall, when Transformer—

When he just.

TRACTION

Upon returning from the hospital, Flowers delivers the news. "They placed him in traction." Broken and fractured, he's a real puzzle. Visits are out of the question. Good. I couldn't go.

"Traction" sounds awful. Later that night at the kitchen table when Flowers describes the pulley system, the appalling logic of that type of equipment makes me want to hide. Not Candy. Candy is fuming. Just fuming. Transformer's vow of silence, his sadness meter, his flesh burning, and cutting, all "his antics." And now this. From where she sits, Transformer is the household deceiver. With worries about Mormor, the selfish one has gone and done something stupid and point-less to grab the spotlight. He's turned everything into some-thing about him. Traction is just the beginning of what we're still learning. He's a bloody mess. There is internal bleeding from his spleen, and a subarachnoid hemorrhage. Medical terms that are hard to swallow. He's got it all.

"After the surgery they induced a coma."

"Does that mean he's asleep?" I squeak.

"Kind of. But not exactly. He's unconscious."

"What the difference?"

"I can't answer that," Flowers says.

"For how long?"

And now Candy lets out a squeal. After holding on to the edges of the tabletop with clenched fingers, she shudders. "Oh sweetie."

Candy shakes her head as if to say, "Do not 'Oh sweetie' me. Do not. Don't you dare." I sense they've already had words. They've talked and set boundaries. There was a conversation, maybe on the phone, from which I was excluded because they probably think I am too young to understand. But I understand. I understand there'll be no Station 10. I understand the band is on an extended hiatus. Why? Because my big brother has gone and done something real. He isn't talking about it. For the time being, he is sleeping on it. People have always said we have telepathy, that we can read each other's minds. But that no longer rings true. What was he doing? Where did he go?

Within a few days, we hear more about the afternoon of the accident from Darren and Nick, who'd been with Transformer at the college. Both pay front-door visits, with their parents standing near them like bodyguards. The story goes that after the gang got bored listening to bad synth music, my brother and Nick and Darren climbed to the roof of the admin building. The Willeys were there too, and after the group managed to hoist a couple of bicycles up, they began making their fun, taking turns riding the bikes around. They started doing stunts. Peeling out, burning rubber, popping wheelies. Just hacking around and having fun when Transformer had this brilliant idea. *Let's play chicken.* Race to the end of the roof—the winner the one who stops closest to the edge. Darren and Nick allegedly were not keen. The fearless Willeys were unfazed. The pair of them went at it first: riding straight and pedalling furiously and screaming at the top of their lungs. Only to stop on a dime. Three yards from the edge, at the exact same spot. Twins. Transformer was next. He was pumped. Neither Darren nor Nick wanted any part of this. Transformer said he'd go alone—but it's not a game of chicken if there aren't two racing. Unless there really are two of you. The others watched him as he started up. Racing straight ahead: forward leaning, pedalling, pedalling, and he never stopped. He fell from their sight. Between buildings, into the forty-foot gap. Was he trying to jump between? That's the only thing that made any sense. But it didn't. Make sense. Transformer wasn't riding a motorcycle. There was just him on a crappy ten-speed.

Him in the world of him and him and him.

MISSING

Flowers drifts through the lowlands. She circles room to room through the impossible fog of these days. I stay upstairs in my room all the time. I do my hiding. The phone rings. Time is a cracked ceramic vase. But, outside, the season turns and the world flashes warning signs in orange and red. The leaves fall from the trees and the neighbours are quickly out on the lawn to stuff garbage bags with the sticky decay. The sky is grey, and the wind makes a strange music. This spoiling feeling in my veins. This ragtime of beauty of loss.

There is a missing person. He is missing from this house. In the morning, at breakfast, I expect to find a poster with his face on it on the fridge door.

No one comes to pay a visit meanwhile. Not Darren, not Nick, none of Transformer's new pals. No Julie and her people. Posted mail or the telephone is preferred to the front door. The medium is the message. *We're scared of you. Of coming too near you. Of catching it.* Bethune sends a letter to inquire about my status. (My status is unintelligible.) New School sends a card signed by close to one hundred students, who are ignorant of mitosis and instead taught anarchy, who inquire about Transformer in hospital. (Status unknown.) The envelope is addressed to the Family Lindstrom. (Status dark sun.) Beyond the cabbage casseroles left on the doorstep and multiple offers to chauffeur me to school, there is not much contact from the outside world. No one wants to pry. No one wants to make eye contact or anything like that.

He is missing.

I'm missing weeks of school.

Here she comes again to raise the dead.

"Never stop your music." The sad-eyed lady lingers by the door, the threat of a tight smile—a smile in traction—implanted upon her face.

She simulates calm. She was just passing through. I was on her route, nothing special to say.

"Did anything happen to him at school?"

"Did they pick on him?"

"Should we contact anyone else who might know something?"

"Did he tell you something?"

"Who is this Julie girl?"

"Where does she come from?"

"Something must have happened to him. What did he tell you?"

She won't leave me alone. She stares over at his side of the room, looking for what she blames herself for missing. She looks at the walls, searching for a plausible answer, for a clue that's been lost between Björn Borg and Patti Smith, for whatever it is she tells herself as his mother she should have known about before anyone else. There had to be something. If it wasn't *something* or *someone*, what was it?

TIMING

What eats my conscience is the timing.

"I had to call you."

"Shit. Hombre."

"I know."

"Holy shit. It's good to hear your voice."

That's about all we can say to each other. We stay on the line, but I don't have language for this place.

"Will you call me back?" Spit says.

It's the timing of this: at the very moment Transformer went sailing off the roof, Spit and I were together, flying high in the cinema. While he entertained the dummos with bicycle tricks, I found crazy entertainment with Spit. And within minutes of my returning home, Sister Candy was at the bathroom door screaming for me to open it.

Candy fright-infused, her dread-permeated face foretelling the news.

Him flying off the roof and me soft landing with Spit.

Candy hammering on my skull because he's in hospital.

And now I can't close the door.

"I'm glad you called back."

"Me too."

"What's going on?"

"We're waiting."

"Any news?"

"No. Not yet."

"Are you okay?"

"I think so. I'm talking with my mom a lot about why he moved into the basement. He told me that 'they' had forced him, that 'they' were treating him almost as if he was bad for me."

"What did she say?"

"She said I shouldn't be thinking about that now."

"She's probably right."

"But I can't stop myself thinking about the visits I made to him. I'd knock before. But talking to him wasn't easy. It wasn't the same anymore."

"Because he wasn't himself?"

"He was different. 'How is Flowers doing?' He was curious about the everyday. 'Where is Candy today?' He cared more. 'What's going on upstairs?' Upstairs was a different hemi-sphere. 'What's for dinner?' 'What's on TV?' 'What's happening at Bethune?'"

"It doesn't sound like him," Spit says.

"Everybody told me he was resting. But from what? He was in bed all the time. 'He needs time,' they said."

"You're doing a lot of thinking, Hombre."

"I guess I understood that something was wrong. Between his vow, his thingamajig, the belly burning. There was lots going on."

"Did you ever ask him?" Spit says.

The killer is "no."

VOICES

Nobody's home but me. I let the phone ring in Flowers' bedroom. I figure it must be his or my school calling again. New School calling "to extend their support" during these difficult times.

It rings a fifth time. *Sorry for your troubles.* A sixth time. *Sorry for the little monster.* A seventh. *Sorry for the mess you're in.* The eighth time and I'm up to grab it.

"This is Megan."

Beside the handset on the nightstand is a photograph of my father in a paisley shirt, beside him Flowers is beginning to show.

"I got the demo."

"Oh."

I turn the portrait so they can't watch me. Then back around.

"Bad timing?"

"How did you find me?"

Weeks ago, we dropped the first tape into the mailbox. Meanwhile, Earth spun off its axis. Duncan McClaren worked his no-number magic after all. Too late.

"It wasn't easy."

MUSIC FOR ALL OCCASIONS

"But I'm a reporter. I've seen you both a few times around town. Outside Station 10 was the last time."

"We were getting out more and more," I say.

"I heard about your brother. And his accident."

He's bloody famous.

"Should I call back? I was just phoning to say how much I like your music. I had a tough time tracking you down, you are right about that, but I wanted to let you know. I thought, well I hoped it might make a difference. Especially now. I hope you don't stop."

I'm not registering much, but Megan's voice makes my face warm.

"I'm going to pitch my editor… Are you still there?"

Barely.

She rattles off a phone number. "And oh yeah, sorry for asking so many questions, but was that a girl's voice on the recording?"

"That's Spit." Downstairs, the front door cracks open, and in a different time zone deliberate footsteps are taking the stairs.

"How do you spell that?"

Flowers stands in the doorway, staring past me at the photograph.

"Who are you talking to?"

I'm on the bed.

"A reporter."

Phone lying by the side of my head.

"Hang up please."

Don't tell me. I'm beside myself.

SOBBING

We've always had our way of being in each other's company, a silent way that doesn't ask much.

When I was seven or eight, one night I got up in the night and found her kneeling by the side of her empty bed. Seeing her like that, I rubbed my eyes and asked if *we* believed in God. She answered my big question by saying she was thinking. She was not in prayer, she was thinking. She made no attempt to explain how it worked, but I grasped the basics: she was thinking of those she loved, in our family. She brought them to mind, one by one, and then… she let them… go?

"Honey."

She let them go, but to where? Back to their own life? Back to their own troubles? I can't stop my sobbing. Life is sad as hell. It really is. It never was before.

"The thing is," I say, "I'm really angry at him."

"You're not alone. So am I."

"You are?"

"Try not to be." She brushes my bangs with a slow hand. "We were all so worried. For such a long time."

"I know," I say, without really feeling it.

"I visited the school to explain that we are keeping things very small and private. That we won't hold a public event. We have our plans, and we're going ahead and having the ceremony downstairs in the living room. They understand our need for privacy. I hope you understand that too."

By now I understand we have no plans to mark my brother's death except to place a circle of chairs in the living room. I understand we are going to play music and read poems and talk about Transformer and say things about life. I understand the time bomb was him after all. It sounds like putting on a play. And I don't have the stage presence for it.

"Is it allowed?"

"Honey, what do you mean?"

"I mean not going to a church, not holding a public funeral. Is it legal?"

"Yes. And don't you worry about the day," Flowers says. "What is most important will be us coming together as a family. You understand, don't you?" She wipes a tear from my eye before it drops. "Life wouldn't be worth living if we didn't have feelings. Now I remember why I came looking for you. Your sister said you were thinking of playing a new song. Were you really?"

"Mostly because I won't be able to say anything without breaking down."

"What's it called?"

"Swedish Boats."

"Swedish Boats," she repeats the name. "I'm happy to hear that. So, you'll perform?"

The song is the first I've written and completed on my own, without putting it through the old Transformer as part of the process. The lyrics are not about Transformer, though. *Swedish Boats, what port is this?* The song is about Morfar and his band of sailors setting a bonfire on the top deck of a company ship.

"Is that a true story?" I ask.

"Yes, it is."

"How do you know?"

"Don't be upset with everyone," she says, "and begin to doubt everything."

"I'm not."

"He was a restless boy, your grandfather. He lived a full life before meeting and marrying your Mormor, and they had their own time and experiences before they had me and your uncle."

Oh, I want to believe that people like me are rooted in things like family, rooted in stories going back sometimes hundreds of years or more, but I feel lost. *My ship is beginning to list.*

"Can I invite Spit?"

"You mean to be at the house?"

"To sing with me."

"I don't know."

"Why not? She was in the band too. I need someone to accompany me."

"Have you talked to her mother about it?" Spit's mother is hardly ever at home. Anyway, why would I talk to her about it?

"I'll promise you one thing," Flowers says. "If you sing your song, he will be there listening. Isn't that enough? I'm sure you want to sing it for him. You'll be relieved and appreciate that you did it. Why not play it alone for him, and for Morfar and Mormor too? For everybody. Will you do that?"

He'll be listening. Sure. Dead listening.

NOMAD

The phone cord is twisted down my arm and around my wrist.

"*Have you talked to her mother?* That's what she said."

"*My* mother? She said that? Are you sure?"

"Yeah. It was weird." I pull at the cord and flex at the elbow until the coils begin to tighten past comfortable and my skin tingles. At least I feel something.

"I don't think I could be there anyway, Hombre," Spit says. "It's freaking me out. Everything is. This whole thing. I've never been to someone's memorial. Plus we're moving."

So that's it. Things go on over my head all the time, but I had a feeling something else huge was in the air.

"I dreamt you were moving," I say. "Where to? Antarctica?"

"I wish."

I've lost another in the mist.

"You're being serious?"

"Yeah. We move around a lot."

Sure, Spit and her mom, they keep moving from place to place to keep things interesting or because they're nomads.

"You've only been in Dorval one year."

"Yeah. I know," she says. "But it's for my mom. To get away. Paul is staying put. We're moving to Halifax. Next time

I'm not going with her. I'll escape to the South Pole for good. I don't want the pressure of making new friends ever again. Look what happened this time. I feel like wherever I go, something goes wrong. Next time, Antarctica, where I'll be alone."

"I bet some Norwegian explorer finds you. With a pack of dogs."

"Me and the mad dogs eat the explorer."

"I'll miss you."

"Better you keep a distance."

Funny.

"We should get off the phone," Spit says.

Automatically I tighten the macaroni vine around my arm until my skin goes red and my fist turns white. I hate not knowing what to say. Silence doesn't stop time.

"Wait a second," she says, and she drops out for about fifteen seconds. "Sorry." Her tone is different upon return.

"What about you, Hombre? Seriously. We haven't really talked about it. How are you doing? This is all crazy."

"You don't have to call me that anymore."

"I guess not."

"It was kind of stupid. The names."

"I didn't mind it." Her voice breaks. The ice cover cracks. I'm going under, watching the air bubbles escape through her hair.

"Wait." I can't stand it. "Can I come over?"

"Right now?"

Now or never.

In no time, I'm through the birds and waiting outside her door, guitar case in hand, feeling sympathy for those in sales, for those poor souls who paste smiles on their faces while knocking at the abyss.

We go straight to her room.

"He'll have to come down." I gesture to the poster of her golden boy, Robbie Pant. The poser from Birmingham.

"Never," she says.

And for once, I laugh. And I don't know why, but I say, "It's good to laugh."

"You never laugh," Spit says.

"I'm stupid like that."

"You should be crying," she says. And I know I should be, she's right. But I cried most of last week. I cried this morning. Cried last night. Crying is for babies, Transformer always said. Crying, taking hugs and love, everything people really need to survive is for babies only. Instead of crying, I'm tuning my guitar.

"You're flat," she says. "Give it over."

My guitar still whiffs of glue and has no weight, feels hollow as theft as I pass it into her hands.

"That reporter from the *Chronicle* called me and asked about the demo."

"Really?" Her eyes flash. "Is she doing an article?"

"I'm not sure. A lot's happening at once."

"No kidding." She shifts over towards me so now we're sitting cross-legged and facing each other. "Sorry. That sounded shitty." She taps my leg. "That reporter's cute. But too old for you. Sometimes we don't notice things." Tugs at her sleeve. "I was just a baby when I got here."

She chewed her bangs when she arrived in Canada; she was small, but not a baby. I know the story. It's one of the first things she told us. It didn't seem important at the time.

"You've been lucky until now."

Lucky? I don't know. Am I supposed to feel guilty? She hands me back my guitar and I futz to get comfortable with it in my lap.

"Go ahead and play," Spit says.

I feel rubbery as I hit the first chord hard. The song is supposed to have the feel of a folk ballad. A ballad or a dirge with hidden teeth. I'm playing it loud and jerky.

"I can't…"

She reaches for her own guitar. "Slow it down and just sing it."

Take me along, I'm not feeling strong,
Take me to where I belong.

"Keep going."

Take me and teach me the words
To your song, I'll sing along.

I rush into the chorus.

Oh, I will follow you,
you with an ancient name.
Yes, I will follow you
where love is no game.

She touches me on the arm. "You're shaking."

"I can't help it."

"It's good, really. I mean, it's beautiful. But it doesn't really sound like you." She pulls the blanket off the top of her bed. "How's that?" she says.

"I feel like Superman."

"You are, Hombre." We're back to that, are we? Spit and Hombre.

"From the top," she says, and soon we have a good grip on the melody. And now for the bridge.

Swedish boats, what port is this?
I have lost you in the mist.
In the waves my ship is beginning to list.

"It's about Transformer, right? And your grandfather?"

She's right. It is about Transformer. And it is about Morfar. Although really it could be about anybody. It could be about Mormor. It could be about Spit herself. Or it could be about me, Hombre. I haven't figured it out.

"Do you have an ending?"

What port is this?
What port is this?
What port is this?

The ending we sing with a slight variation, a minor modulation each time. Over and over until the same words start to mean something different.

At first, it doesn't make sense seeing everybody sitting in a circle on the kitchen chairs in the living room. It starts when Candy says, "I'll go. Close your eyes."

Everybody in the room probably has their own sadness meter and is using it now.

"It's by an Italian composer called Albinoni. This is his funeral march."

Albinoni is cruel music. Where did she get this? Albinoni is pure torture. Some music upon first listen doesn't touch me. Not Albinoni. Albinoni is sad and a bit corny. But in minutes it tears me apart. The experience is like having the composer come inside to film a motion picture of my heart. With music like this, the damage is done before you become wise to it. Cut away, cut to Morfar and Mormor who are leaning on each other while listening to cruel Albinoni. Cut to Flowers and Candy who are sobbing. The music is a family drama composed of organ and cello, and of the violin that goes searching for the saddest note on earth but never really finds it. Uncle Per is watching something out the front double windows when the needle lifts. He selects a different record.

Good riddance. Albinoni ravaged us. Uncle Per now begins talking. "In his too brief life, he only looked forward. Transformer, this music is a soundtrack to *Doctor Zhivago*, a movie set during the Russian revolution." He looks straight at me. "Your brother wanted things to change. I just wish he had been more patient. More careful."

Is it about movies today? *Doctor Zhivago* was no part of our inheritance. What's the connection? Years ago, when it came on television, Flowers told us it was one of my father's favourite movies and that we were supposed to read the book when we got older. The music alienates me until we get to the overture. And I realize this is winter music. Winter music makes sense. Cut to the Tomten on the kitchen walls at Christmas and the table set with plates of pickled herring and squat shot glasses filled to the brim with aquavit, and I see that Morfar and Mormor are about to rise out of their chairs to sing a round of "Helan Går."

Isn't Flowers going to say or read something? I close my eyes and wait. Joni Mitchell's singing startles me. If we cried to Albinoni and *Doctor Zhivago*, what's going to happen now? We're going to be broken into pieces and admitted to hospital and put in traction like Transformer was so nobody can move again.

"You can stop it," Flowers directs Uncle Per to lift the needle. "I have no magic words. I feel pain. It's unfair. I'm still angry. I don't want to be. I love everybody in this room. Your father wanted to take care of you. All of you."

Flowers is standing.

"He was frightened that he would not see any of you grow up. He didn't feel…"

She's onto the founding myth and the family's fragility is getting put on a platter, but for some reason, with my eyes closed, I anticipate a variation.

"You see, he had a heart murmur and there were complications. Despite this, he wanted children in part because when he was a child he was placed in foster care. He did the rounds of that circuit until he landed with an older couple in Minneapolis. He was never that close to his adopted parents. I met them only once. By then they were living in Duluth, and your father claimed he would only visit them there because it was the birthplace of Bob Dylan. So off we went and spent a weekend with them, and some years later we discovered that his own birth mother was living in San Francisco, and that was the reason for our trip west."

It was the reason for the nightstand photograph of my parents taken at the intersection of Haight and Ashbury.

"We were hippies before it all got started. We travelled in a VW. For myself, it was a chance to retrace Morfar's footsteps. When your Morfar first arrived in America, he coached tennis on Long Island but then left for California and found work on a fruit farm. This was during the Great Depression. In the end, he left America and returned to Sweden to marry Mormor. You're probably asking yourself why I'm repeating this now. It's because this morning when I thought about what I would say, I could only think of the things I don't want you to ever forget... and... I want you to know... you both and your brother... you all come from... I just wish..."

She sits down. It's not fair. Nobody can talk about him, really. Uncle Per puts on the next selection, and Flowers' second choice of music is "Bleecker Street." The earnestness of Simon & Garfunkel makes me feel embarrassed. But I know *Wednesday Morning, 3 A.M.* is like religion to Flowers. I used to spend a lot of time trying to tell them apart by studying their faces on the album cover. Which one is Paul Simon? Art Garfunkel? What kind of name is Art? I was drawn to the photograph of the duo standing on the station platform with the warm orange blur of a subway train passing through— that made a lot of sense to me when I first heard this music. The photograph has them busking, but not really, since they are both too aware of the camera.

My turn. This will be my second real gig. If you want, you can call this busking, go ahead. I'm thinking of subway trains and of light travelling through us at speed. I'm thinking of Transformer and myself standing in the warm Atwater metro station, looking down the line for something that doesn't appear. Cut away then to us at the bottom of the street waiting in the bus shelter and Transformer doing his jerky "Let them eat kaka!" dance around and around the little fire. Cut away to Flowers and the Swedes taking summer sun. Cut away to Candy sitting beside her colonel at the Vets, helping him to a lungful of poisonous history. Cut back to the location of the bus shelter and the two figures looking back in time. Cut to his eyes as dull as weak headlights. Close curtain on our dead souls.

Afterwards, Morfar comes around to me, and I stand to receive him.

"Thank you for singing," Morfar says. "That was brave."

Dorval, good night! This is it. The crowd will always want more. An encore. But the lads are backstage, diving into limos already. The motorcade leaves the underground parking garage to the drift of melancholy strains. The taillights leech red into the black of night. The minstrels arrive and wait on the tarmac. JFK or LaGuardia. The jet taxies up the runway. The credits roll. The plane lifts off. Into the yonder. Above the clouds. The band is gone, and all we have left is the music. Heartbreaking music that upset our lives.

In front of the mirror, I do away with my guitar.

"The name of this band is Because."

I wonder: did his pant leg get caught on the pedal before he could apply the brake? Has anyone asked that? Did he underestimate his speed? Misjudge the line separating solid surface and air? What about pure goofy recklessness gone wrong? Was he stoned out of his mind? Was he being punk? He swore that punk is about being quiet inside. I'm not convinced.

"Why?"

"Because."

"Because why?"

Because people aren't stars.

Because nobody can read minds.

Because silence is silence.

Epilogue

1998

Calling out in transit, I was busking in the same spot along Saint Laurent Boulevard, and sure the kid returned.

"You were one of the brothers, right?" She waved the cassette in my face.

Without you, Spit, there'd be no tapes, no demo, no fossil record of the band's existence.

"Where did you get that?"

No electromagnetic afterlife.

"It was sent it to my mom before I was born."

"No way." I'm stunned, I mean, dying of laughter inside. Despite the best efforts of our intrepid manager, the music did get around.

"She has a bunch of old tapes. Mostly, it's rare stuff. A lot of bad music. But some is good."

The kid stood for a bit longer on the end of that statement.

"That's lucky," I said.

"She's really into the angry girl who sings '*Antarctica! Antarctica!*' We have an inside joke at home about that. Mom likes to sing loud when she's frustrated. '*Antarctica! Antarctica! Do not pass 'Go'! Straight to the fat farm!'* My brother and I play along sometimes. It's like a house standard. *'It's time to move to Antarctica!'"*

"So who is this mom of yours?"

She grimaced, soured on me. Was it realizing that she was in a conversation with a faded, thirty-something busker?

"She's… my mom! She stays home with my brother."

"Ah. And before that?"

"Her job?" Chagrin; not interested. "Graphics. Before that a journalist."

"Very cool."

She flinched at "cool" and kicked at the ground. I was not cool in her world.

"How old are you again?"

Her face said it: corny asshole.

"Fourteen."

"And you don't play an instrument?" My hands were cold. I was tuning up. This was taking me time.

"You're flat," she said.

"I'm always flat," I said, and she managed a half smile. "You know, you remind me of someone I used to know, someone with a very good ear."

"I bet I know who."

"I bet you do too." At this she smiled. "If I was your age again, I'd ask for that new guitar soon and start playing it right away. For your birthday?"

"I might."

"I can give you lessons. I'm not a technician but—"

"What's a technician?" she interrupted.

"Never mind." I slipped a guitar pick from my pocket.

"Next time we can talk about that."

"Maybe." She was about to go. But had one last question.

"What happened to your band?"

Well, didn't I strike a pose and pretend to have that old-time rock 'n' roll presence? After she left, well, you know the rest. A technician's a dead musician.

Notes and Acknowledgements

All along, I wanted this novel to remain a quiet tribute to the Montreal underground music scene. I was a "member" of that indie scene from the early eighties to the mid-nineties, recording and performing with two bands, Weather Permitting and the Good Cookies. While the main action of the novel is set primarily in 1981, many of the Montreal bands referenced in these pages were most active from 1983 to 1990 and beyond. In fact, a few are still making music today. I tried to preserve my own memories within these pages and, in some instances, the personalities from a community that I cherish still—but, in a work of fiction, without finally upholding historical accuracy. In so doing, I made a lot of people so much younger than they were then and older than they really are now.

I owe my memories of that certain time and place to many people. The few listed here include dear friends and some relative strangers, dead and alive: Donna Lee Marsh, Steve Burliuk, Rob Drummond, Frank Criniti, Mack MacKenzie, Stewart MacKenzie, Patti Schmidt, Chris Burns, Mark Lepage, Duncan McTavish, Martin Siberok, Peter McGoldrick, Brent Bambury, Matthew Dupuis, Gerard van Herk, Paul Gott, Rob

Costain, Annabel Busby, Brian Busby, Rob Labelle, Andrew Frank, Mike Webber, Gary McGirr, Bruno Steiner, Robert Berry, Clara Gabriel, Gabriela O'Connor, Alen Mattich, Owen Egan, Steve Sinclair, Ron Woo, Adrian West, Donna Varicca, Morris Appelbaum, Ian Stephens, Alex Soria, and Kim Shadow.

Deep gratitude to my editor, Dimitri Nasrallah, for making this novel sound like it should. Thanks to Simon Dardick, Nancy Marrelli, Carmine Starnino, and Jennifer Varkonyi at Véhicule Press, and thanks to David Drummond for the inspired book cover. I wouldn't have got this far without my writing pals, Missy Marston and David O'Meara, who, since this novel was in demo form, inspired me to get a tune out of it. Thank you both so much. Deep gratitude to Jeff Miller and Peter Steinmetz for the close reads. Jill, Sonya, and Emil, you three are the power trio who sustain me day and night, night and day.

This novel is dedicated in loving memory to my grandparents, Orvar and Berta Lindstrom. Morfar and Mormor, your soul music stirs me.

ESPLANADE
Books